SECRETS OF THE DEEP

Also by Danielle Singleton:

Safe & Sound
Do No Harm (Joseph #1)
The Enemy Within (Joseph #2)
The Containment Zone
Price of Life

Connect with the author online:

www.daniellesingleton.com
@auntdanwrites
www.facebook.com/singletondanielle
www.daniellesingleton.wordpress.com

Secrets of the Deep

Danielle Singleton

This book is a work of fiction and any resemblance to persons, living or dead, or places, events, or locales is purely coincidental. The characters are productions of the author's imagination and used fictitiously.

ISBN: 1530230020

Original cover image: © Dabarti CGI (license purchased)

*****

To Gran and MamaLynn:
For The Love

"A grandmother is a little bit parent, a little bit
teacher, and a little bit best friend."
~Anonymous

ACKNOWLEDGMENTS

This list begins and ends with Jesus Christ. Without Him, I am nothing. With Him, I can do anything.

Thank you to my family and friends for putting up with me and my crazy story ideas, frustrated rants, and (at times) near-obsessive behavior. There's no way I could be on Book #6 already without your support!

A very large thank you, as always, to the dedicated and hardworking members of my Reading Committee. I write stories but y'all help turn them into books, and for that you have my undying gratitude.

Thank you to Dave Hurley and the Arvid family (Thomas, Vanessa, Jimmy, and Christopher) for allowing me to come aboard *The Salesmanship* this past summer. Believe it or not, that was the inspiration for this book! Thanks also to Anya and Ryan at Dolphin Cay (Atlantis Bahamas) for your kind hospitality to my family and me, and to Brooke Patterson for your help with all things fashion-related.

To Dennis and Cindy O'Keefe, Mark and Mary Jo Kovacs, and the Van Horn, Hatcher, and Blankenship families – thank you for your ongoing friendship and support of my writing endeavors.

And, as always, thank you ever so much to Gus. It's amazing how much four paws and a tail can do to bring light, love, and laughter into one's life. Te amo mijo.

I hope y'all enjoy the story!

Secrets of the Deep

*****

"Very few of us are what we seem."

Agatha Christie

ONE

"What are you hiding?"

Thomas Wilson stopped what he was doing and turned to face his wife, MaryJo, who was standing in the bedroom doorway of their Manhattan home.

"Nothing," Thomas replied, calling on his decades of experience in the business world to remain calm under pressure.

MaryJo, for her part, relied upon her experience as Thomas' wife to know when he was lying.

"I heard the bottles clanging," she said. "And saw you shoving things into your carry-on, trying to hide them before I came in here."

Thomas, still fit and trim at sixty-four, shoved his hands into the pockets of his khaki slacks and shrugged his shoulders, his pressed green golf shirt rising and falling with them.

"I don't know what you're talking about. I'm not hiding anything."

MaryJo strode across the large master bedroom, looking every inch the millionaire's wife in her Jimmy Choo stiletto heels and matching Chanel pantsuit. She pushed her husband to the side so she could see what was in his black weekender.

Unzipping the bag, she counted two bottles of scotch and one of vodka.

"There's already more than enough alcohol on the boat. Or are you to the point where you can't survive a three hour flight without a drink?"

"I don't have to go three hours. There's liquor on the plane. These are just in case."

"Just in case of what?" MaryJo asked, sharpening her tone and putting her hands on her slender hips. Although she was fifty-nine, Mrs. Wilson's trainer kept her looking at least ten years younger. "Just in case the plane crashes and we're

1

stranded on an island somewhere?"

Thomas grinned, the same crooked half-smile that closed thousands of business deals and made MaryJo fall in love with and marry him thirty-seven years earlier.

"It could happen," he replied, still grinning.

This time the smile wasn't working.

"You're unbelievable," MaryJo snapped, irritated by her husband's newfound drinking hobby.

Thomas stepped closer to the bed and looked down at his wife, his tall frame towering over hers. "And you," he said, leaning down an inch from her face, "need to mind your own damn business."

He picked his wallet off the nightstand and shoved it in his back pocket.

"Where are you going now?"

"To the office. Where else?" Thomas replied, shouldering past his wife to exit the room.

"We're leaving for the airport at two!" MaryJo called out behind him. "Don't be late!"

Jogging down the staircase of his five-story townhouse, Thomas reached the foyer and headed toward the front door.

"Will you need the car, sir?"

Thomas jumped in surprise. "Woah, Mason, didn't see you there. No," he told the butler, "I'll walk."

Leaving his house, Thomas Wilson headed north on 3rd Avenue in the opposite direction of his office. At 6'1" with a slim but athletic build, it was never a surprise when people learned that he played sports in college. Tennis was his game of choice, to the point that Tom imitated his forehand and backhand swings while venturing farther and farther north in the Upper East Side. His dark gray hair still had a few sprinkles of black, and deep brown eyes complemented his megawatt smile as he greeted passersby.

When he reached 79th Street and turned right, Thomas Wilson II looked like a walking Brooks Brothers ad, with the confidence of one born into wealth and the subtle swagger of a man who took a comfortable living and turned it into a fortune. Tom was straight from central casting for 'New York banker', and he embraced the role. Perfectly tailored dark suits lined his closet for weekdays, while a steady diet of khakis, loafers, and polo shirts filled his weekend attire. Today's look was no exception.

Reaching his destination, Tom bounded up the steps two at a time and pushed open the heavy mahogany doors of St. Monica's Church.

TWO

Halfway down the center aisle of St. Monica's stunning gothic cathedral, the parish priest was restocking prayer books in advance of that night's Saturday mass.

"Good morning, Padre. Need any help?"

"Ah, Tom, you're here," Father Gerry Napier replied, calling the parishioner by his more common name. Only Mrs. Wilson called her husband Thomas. "Sure, I'd love some help if you have time. I need to finish filling in these front rows."

When the last prayer books were placed on the softly carved wooden pews, Father Gerry turned to Tom and smiled. "Thanks. That went much faster with an extra set of hands."

"Tom and Gerry, at it again. Except you're Gerry with a G."

The priest's laughter echoed off the cavernous walls of the church. "Tom and Gerry. I like it. I wasn't sure I'd see you today since your family is leaving for vacation this afternoon."

"Yeah, well, I knew I'd miss next week for sure so I figured I'd squeeze in one more trip if I could."

"Come on back to my office. We can talk there."

Walking ahead of his frequent penitent, Gerry Napier couldn't help but reflect on the difference between the man in his church and the man the rest of the world thought they knew. Tom Wilson's charitable work, devotion to his family, business success, and squeaky clean image should have made him the man who cynical New Yorkers loved to hate, but deep down even the most jaded of Manhattanites liked and respected the renowned investment banker. *I mean, just last week he was featured in the New York Times Magazine,* Gerry thought. *'How to build an empire, raise a family, and look great while doing it'.* The priest shook his head. *I can*

4

only imagine what they'd say if they knew that Tom Wilson was also a budding alcoholic and came here once a week for counseling. To say nothing of everything he's confessed to me.

The two men entered Father Gerry's office and closed the door behind them.

"Have a seat," the pastor said, gesturing toward Tom's usual chair. "So . . . you head out later today?"

"Yep. We're leaving the house at two. Wheels up at Teterboro at three."

"I thought you might've flown commercial since the whole family is going."

"Nah. With nine people, including two young kids, it's way easier to fly private."

Father Gerry nodded his head as if he understood, but in reality the idea of spending $50,000 on a single flight was mind-boggling. *Especially when commercial could get them there for under $8,000.*

"No TSA, no two-bag limit," Tom continued. "Although, based on what MaryJo had laid out for her suitcases, we might go over the weight limit for the plane. She's bringing eight pairs of shoes, Padre. To spend ten days on a boat on which you aren't allowed to wear shoes."

"That certainly does sound like Mrs. Wilson," Gerry said with a smile, although he'd never met the woman. MaryJo and the rest of Tom's family knew nothing about his visits to St. Monica's.

"This trip will be good for you," the priest added. "It'll give you some time away from normal life here and will let you and MaryJo and your kids reconnect."

Tom focused his attention on a scuff mark on the thigh of his pants. Rubbing it with his thumb, he replied: "yeah, maybe. Or we could get so irritated being in such close quarters that we kill each other by the end of the week."

"Tom . . ." Gerry said slowly.

"What?"

"We're thinking positive thoughts, right?"

Wilson sighed. "Right. Positive thoughts. Good trip. It'll be a good trip."

"That's better. How was your week, by the way?"

"I thought you said only positive thoughts in here," Tom quipped. The millionaire businessman resumed picking at the stain on his pant leg. "I can't figure out what this is," he said, avoiding the priest's question.

"Tom . . ."

"You sound like my grandmother when you say my name like that."

"Grandmothers are wonderful people," the middle-aged pastor replied with a smile. "A good number of my parishioners here are grandmothers who are raising three, four, or five grandkids on their own."

Sensing an opportunity to change the subject, Tom looked across the desk at the priest. "Is there any way I can help? You know I'm active with a lot of charitable boards in the city."

"Our parish has already benefitted immensely from your generosity, Mr. Wilson. Now I want you to benefit from this conversation by telling me how your week was."

"My liquor cabinet is 5 bottles lighter," Tom said with a sardonic smile. "Aside from that, pretty much the same as the week before."

"You really need to cut back on your drinking, Tom."

"And now you sound like my wife."

The priest leaned back in his chair and folded his arms across his chest, waiting for his guest's anger to subside. *Always the same*, Gerry thought. *Delay, avoid, delay, avoid, fight, fight, fight . . . and then finally open up for about a minute and a half before leaving.*

Tom Wilson let out a heavy sigh and sank down in his own chair. "When I drink, my brain slows down. It doesn't think as much. I can focus on the whisky and the glass and the music playing in the background, and for a little while at least I can forget about the fact that I'm a complete fuck-up and going to burn in Hell." He paused. "Plus, if I don't drink then I can't sleep. And if I can't sleep then I can't function the next day at work." Tom's sly smile returned. "It's medicinal, Padre. A fifth of scotch at night, every night, as needed."

Gerry shook his head. "That's not good for you. You're going to ruin your liver."

Tom shrugged. "The only other cure would be coming clean. It's far better for me to have cirrhosis than my family to know what kind of person I really am."

"The truth will come out eventually, Tom."

Wilson lifted his head up with a jerk and glared at the man sitting across the desk from him. "No it won't. Not as long as I have anything to say about it, it won't. It can't."

THREE

Sixteen blocks away at the Wilson residence, in a far more affluent area of the city, MaryJo had resumed packing for the family's ten day cruise around the Caribbean. It was a Wilson tradition. At the end of July, when most of their friends in New York left for the Hamptons, Tom, MaryJo, and their kids spent a week and a half sailing around the Bahamas on their yacht.

MaryJo was looking forward to this year's trip, particularly since her daughter and son-in-law hadn't been able to go the previous year. "Now that Harper is fifteen months, she can join the fun," MaryJo said with a smile, referring to the younger of her two granddaughters.

'MamaJo', as they called her, adored her daughter's little girls and couldn't wait until more grandkids arrived. Although she was raised in New York, MaryJo was the daughter of a Southern debutante and carried with her many of the character traits that earned her ancestors the title of steel magnolias. Kind and compassionate yet principled and strong-willed, Mrs. Wilson was the perfect complement to her hard-charging and gallant husband. Indeed, they were New York society's model couple: married thirty-seven years with three children and zero scandals to their name.

"Zero scandals for now," MaryJo muttered as she continued folding piles of Dior, Gucci, and Hermés and placing them into suitcases. "That won't last long if he keeps drinking like this." She stopped packing and sat down on the edge of her bed.

I wish he'd tell me what's wrong, she thought. *He's never been like this before.*

The unexpected change in behavior was what bothered MaryJo the most. If Thomas had always been a drinker, or always been moody and secretive, she would know how to handle it. But her husband's steady demeanor and sterling reputation were part of what attracted her to him in the first place. With degrees from Harvard and Wharton and a solid job lined up in Thomas Sr.'s investment firm, the young Thomas II had been a catch. *Still is*, his wife thought. *Even like this.*

A knock on the bedroom door shook MaryJo back to the present.

"Excuse me, ma'am?" asked the family's longtime housekeeper, Mrs. Mason.

"Yes?"

"Mr. Mason would like to know if your things are ready to go downstairs," she said, referring to her husband, the butler.

"Not yet. Give me another twenty minutes or so."

After the housekeeper nodded and left, MaryJo stood up from the bed and resumed packing. "Maybe this trip will be good for us," she said to herself. "Maybe by the end of it, the old Thomas will be back."

****

Twenty-five miles away in the wealthy bedroom community of Purchase, New York, Thomas Wilson III and his wife Anya were busy putting the finishing touches on their own travel bags. Tripp, as he was known, was a junior partner at his father's firm in Midtown, but he didn't mind the commute into the city every day. The thirty-five year old had always preferred the slower pace of life in the suburbs, and he was thrilled that his wife agreed with him.

Anya Wilson, née Dubois, viewed her quiet suburban life as a slice of paradise. The daughter of a Foreign Service officer, she was born in New York but raised in various cities in Europe and was more than happy to set down roots in the Westchester County hamlet of Purchase. Especially since the tiny but tony shopping district there offered her a chance to open her own clothing boutique.

9

Married five years earlier after meeting on a flight from Zurich to London, Tripp and Anya had more than their fair share of arguments in the first few years of marriage – mostly due to what they called 'cultural differences'.

"You can't honestly expect me to feel comfortable having some stranger living in my house all the time and waiting on me hand and foot," Anya often yelled.

Tripp, having grown up with live-in servants, never understood the problem. "They're not strangers – they're staff. And you have to be the only woman in America who wouldn't want somebody else to do the cooking and cleaning every day."

In the end, Anya acquiesced to the expectations of her in-laws' world – although the housekeeper didn't live-in and only worked 10 – 4. Nevertheless, since her marriage to Tripp, Anya Wilson had resolved to become a picture-perfect society wife, something that was beginning to grate on her husband.

"Don't you care about anything aside from clothes?" he asked as he walked into Anya's dressing room and saw a half-dozen suitcases covering the floor.

The thirty-two year old glared at her husband and put her hands on her waifish hips. Although she was nearing her second trimester of pregnancy, the model-thin mom-to-be had yet to start showing.

"When you go to an event or a meeting or are photographed for the society pages, what do they ask you about? Your job. Your activities. It will say 'Thomas Wilson III, junior partner at Wilson|Cole'," she added, displaying the titles in air quotes with her hands. "Do they ask me about my clothing store? My involvement with youth literacy campaigns? No," Anya said, shaking her head. "It's always: 'Anya, who are you wearing? Where'd you find that handbag? Anya Wilson in Alexander McQueen'.

"I care about fashion, dear husband, because I have to care about fashion. Honestly, I don't give a shit. Give me

J.Crew and some Lily Pulitzer in the summer and I'm happy. The clothes I design and sell in my store are decidedly not haute couture. But jeans and a t-shirt aren't acceptable for Anya Wilson of the New York Wilsons. If *I* didn't care about fashion, *we* would be a laughing stock. And your mom and sister would pitch a fit." She paused and took a deep breath. "So no, Tripp, a shoe isn't just a shoe. Sometimes, a shoe is your whole damn personal image wrapped into a peep-toe and stiletto heel."

Tripp rolled his eyes and sighed, having stopped listening when she started name-dropping designers. "And sometimes, babe," he said, "it's just a shoe. Hurry up and finish packing – we need to leave for my parents' soon."

FOUR

Later that day, nine Wilsons and twenty-two bags of luggage piled into three Uber SUVs for the short ride from Manhattan to Teterboro Airport.

"Where Gus?" asked Madison, Tom and MaryJo's precocious granddaughter.

Madison's mom, Kay, smiled and rubbed her daughter's arm. "I told you, honey, Gus isn't coming on the boat."

"Why didn't you bring him?" asked Luke, Kay's husband and Madison's father.

"It's too much of a hassle," replied MaryJo, speaking of her beloved chocolate lab. "I'd have to line up all of his vaccine forms ahead of time and find a vet to examine him when we got to the Bahamas. Plus, he'd go stir-crazy on the boat for that long without being able to run around."

"He'll have a great time with Mr. and Mrs. Mason," Tom added, repeating the words he said minutes earlier when bidding goodbye to the eighty pound bundle of fur.

"Won't you, big guy?" he had said, rubbing behind the dog's ears.

Gus responded by licking his owner underneath the chin.

"At least he didn't get my mouth," Tom reminisced with a laugh.

Madison, for her part, crossed her tiny arms in her car seat and sulked. "I want Gus."

"You'll see him in ten days," her mother said. "And, in the meantime, you get to be with all of us."

****

Four hours later, after an uneventful flight aboard a rented Challenger 350, the Wilsons were back in SUVs and riding along the narrow two-lane road that led from Nassau's airport to Atlantis Harbor. Most of Tom and MaryJo's friends docked their yachts in St. Bart's or the Cayman Islands, but the Wilsons preferred the calmer pace of The Exumas and other lower Bahamian islands.

"Everywhere else is too crowded," Tom liked to say. "I go on vacation to get away from my friends and co-workers, not to see them every night at dinner."

Tom, MaryJo, and their two granddaughters were in the first car, along with the majority of the luggage. Madison, at three and a half years old, was curious about everything – her every fifth word was 'why'. With her dad's wavy blonde hair and her mom's brown eyes, Maddy was the ultimate girly girl and apple of her grandfather's eye.

"We're going to have so much fun, aren't we?" Tom said, smiling at his firstborn grandchild.

"Mmm hmm!"

In the car seat next to Madison sat Harper: fifteen months and going on fifteen years. In contrast to her sister, Harper inherited her mom's brown hair and her dad's blue eyes. She was, without a doubt, the most beautiful member of the Wilson family.

"She's going to be a heartbreaker one day," Tom said.

"And a ball-buster," MaryJo added. Unlike her dainty sister, Harper was a loud, adventurous, rough-and-tumble toddler.

"All the better," their grandfather replied. "She'll need to be to keep the dogs away."

"We get dog?!"

"No honey. I was talking about something else."

Madison frowned and turned as far as her car seat would allow so she could look out the window at the ocean as they drove by.

"Did you get everything settled at the office this morning?"

"Huh?"

"At this office this morning," MaryJo repeated. "You said you needed to make sure everything was set up for you

13

to be gone on vacation."

Tom's mind flashed back to his visit to St. Monica's and the voice of Father Gerry advising him to come clean and tell the truth. *Not now, Padre*, he thought, pushing the priest's image out of his head.

"Yeah, I got it all done," Tom lied. "Charles and the rest of the team will be able to manage everything, and they know they can reach me if it's an absolute, hair-on-fire emergency."

Following behind the first SUV, the rest of the family was piled into what Ryan Wilson called 'the fun car'. Tom and MaryJo's youngest child was fifteen years old and, although he grew six inches since Christmas, the doctors predicted that Ryan might still have another half foot to go before reaching a full height of 6'5". As a consequence, the teenager with a mop of curly brown hair and matching brown eyes resembled a baby horse learning to walk: all arms and legs and fur. Ryan was excited about this vacation because it gave him a chance to prove to his brother and sister that he was mature enough to hang out with them. He was also eager to get to know them better, since both Tripp and Kay moved out of the house before their brother was old enough to spend any quality time with them.

Tripp and Anya were riding beside Ryan on the sideways-facing bench in the stretch-SUV, while the brothers' only sister and her husband were in the forward-facing seats in the far back.

Katherine Wilson Eckersely, 32, was everything a proper, monied New York woman should be. Educated at Dalton and Miss Porter's, Kay's one attempt at rebellion in life was to go to college at Dartmouth instead of her father's alma mater, Harvard. With brown hair and brown eyes like the rest of her family, Kay was tall for a woman – 5'9" – and was big-boned but worked very hard to stay thin. Before getting married, Mrs. Eckersely was an assistant at an art gallery. She recently returned there to volunteer part-time.

The trendy studio fit her style, since Kay knew more about contemporary fashion than the rest of her preppy family combined. A Kappa Kappa Gamma at Dartmouth, Kay met her future husband at a fraternity party her sophomore year. To the dismay of both sets of parents, the pair married two years after graduation.

"Twenty-four is way too young to be getting married," MaryJo had said in a huff while driving home from dinner with the newly-engaged couple.

Her husband scoffed. "You were twenty-two and they called you an 'old bride'."

"Yes, well, I'm Southern. And times are different now."

Tom nodded. "They sure are."

It took several years for Luke Eckersely to gain his in-laws' trust. The same age as his wife, Luke was a consultant for a management firm and an exceptionally handsome man. Tall and fit with wavy blonde hair and blue eyes, he could have made a serious run at a career in modeling if his family would've approved. "He looks like a damn Aryan prototype for the Third Reich," Tripp had whispered to his dad the first time they met Kay's then-boyfriend. Luke was in the Theta Delta fraternity at Dartmouth and was a standard-issue New Jersey prep. The son of a hedge fund manager father and a mother who did lunch, the Eckerselys were not nearly as rich or as charitable as the Wilsons but were still well-off enough to send their only son to The Lawrenceville School to play soccer and lacrosse.

Much to his fashionable wife's delight, Luke announced to the car that he was attempting to grow a beard while on vacation – "even though I'll have to shave it before I go back to work."

Kay looked over at her sister-in-law with excitement in her eyes. "Speaking of things that are growing, have you started thinking about names?"

Anya placed her hand over her still-flat stomach and shook her head. "Not really, or at least I haven't. If it's a boy,

15

Tripp wants to name him Thomas Wilson IV."

Tripp smiled. "Absolutely."

"You can call him Cuatro," said Ryan, and the whole car starting laughing.

The family members were all very excited about Anya's pregnancy, especially knowing how long they had been trying to have a baby. Two weeks earlier at a birthday dinner for MaryJo, the parents-to-be made the announcement.

Clinking his knife against his water glass, Tripp stood up at the dining room table in his parents' home.

"So, we were going to wait until the trip to tell everyone," he said, reaching down to take hold of Anya's hand, "but we're too excited to keep it secret any longer." Tripp smiled. "Anya is pregnant. We're going to have a baby."

MaryJo declared it the best birthday present she'd ever received, and Tom had gone to the bank the next morning to open a trust account for his future grandchild – just as he had done for Madison and Harper before they were born.

In the car on the way to the harbor, Kay pulled her cell phone out of her purse and started scrolling through her list of contacts. "I'll give you the name of the nanny agency," she said. "They're great. Background checks, super professional. Everybody uses them."

"I wasn't planning on having a nanny."

Again, everyone in the car laughed.

"Don't be ridiculous, honey," said Tripp. "Of course we'll have a nanny. Besides, there's no way you could run your clothes shop and watch a baby full-time."

Anya sighed. "That's true."

"Have you registered?" asked Kay.

"For gifts?"

"No, for school."

"Not yet," said Anya. "We're planning to after we get back to New York."

Her sister-in-law shook her head. "You should call and

16

see if you can do it over the phone. At least get your name down. The waitlist can be super long."

"He or she will be a third-generation legacy at Dalton," Tripp replied. "It won't be a problem."

Worry lines creased Anya's forehead. "No, Kay's right. Dalton shouldn't be an issue, but two-year-old preschool could be."

Ryan laughed and was surprised when no one else joined him. "You announced you're pregnant like a week ago and you're already worried about getting the baby into preschool?"

Kay nodded her head, answering on Anya's behalf. "Definitely. To get into the right upper school, you need the right lower school. For that, you need the right kindergarten. And kindergarten admissions are a cut-throat business."

"Even if we're living out in Purchase?" Anya asked.

"If you want him or her to go to high school in the city, you need to start building the résumé now."

Ryan rolled his eyes. *I don't care that I went through that same private school gauntlet when I was a kid*, he thought. *It's still ridiculous.*

A second later, the pink towers of the Atlantis Resort and Paradise Island came into view.

"Oooh hey, there's the harbor!" Ryan called out, his excitement overwhelming his teenage urge to look cool. "Do you see *The Arvid*?"

Joining his brother in looking out the window, Tripp pointed with his finger: "there she is. Second one from the left."

All five passengers in the SUV smiled.

We made it! Kay thought. *Let the vacation begin!*

FIVE

Atlantis Marina was a sixty-three slip luxury harbor adjacent to the Atlantis resort. While it was full of megayachts and their megarich owners, none drew more attention than the one belonging to the Wilsons. *The Arvid* was a 121-foot long navy blue and white beauty with running board panels that lit up and changed colors at night. A PJ 123 motor, FRP Composite hull, and maximum speed of twenty-two knots meant that the yacht could hold its own with any other boat in the harbor – or ocean for that matter. But *The Arvid*'s strength and power didn't hold a candle to its luxurious interior. Leather furniture, central air conditioning, and WiFi covered the whole boat, and a crew of up to six catered to the family members on board.

On the top deck, open to the sun, were a dining table, wet bar, and Jacuzzi. The second level housed an outdoor eating area, indoor dining room, living room, and the master bedroom where Tom and MaryJo slept. Directly off the master bedroom, jutting out the starboard side, was a small, retractable patio where Mr. and Mrs. Wilson could relax undisturbed. Below decks, on the third level, were three additional guest bedrooms and the crew's quarters. It was a tight fit when all nine Wilsons made the trip, but they didn't mind. Kay, Luke, and their two little girls were in the VIP stateroom, Tripp and Anya shared a double cabin room, and Ryan took the other double cabin.

"Things are going to be really cramped when Tripp and Anya's baby is born," Tom commented to his wife as they walked under the pale pink archways of the Atlantis hotel toward the marina.

"Or if Kay has any more kids," MaryJo added.

Tom laughed. "You know what that means, Chief Brody. We're gonna need a bigger boat."

A few minutes later, the family arrived at their yacht.

"I always forget how pretty she is," Tom said with a smile.

"Your most prized possession," his wife commented.

"Nope, that'd be you," he replied and kissed her on the cheek.

Tom took off his brown loafers and placed them in a shoe basket beside the ramp to the boat. "Honey, I'm home," he called out.

Three crew members – two male and one female – emerged from inside the yacht to welcome the Wilsons aboard. Although *The Arvid* was built for a crew of six, Tom Wilson preferred to only carry three: the captain, a first mate, and a cook. "We don't need anybody else," he said.

The cook's duties were self-explanatory, and the middle-aged Jamaican woman preferred to stay in the kitchen away from the boisterous Wilson clan. All of her meals were excellent, though, so the guests and crew were willing to overlook her often gruff demeanor.

The first mate, Marcelo, was a native of the Bahamas who started working on a different boat as a part-time bosun. Over the years he worked himself up to Second Mate, and a year earlier he was hired by the Wilsons as full-time First Mate. "Not bad for a high school dropout," he liked to say.

The heart and soul of *The Arvid*, though, was her captain, Blankenship Jones. Thirty-three years old and leather-tanned from the sun, 'Ship', as he was called, was one of the youngest yet most experienced megayacht captains in the Caribbean. English by birth, Ship's accent was an odd combination of British public schoolboy and island creole, with phrases such as "let 'er rip, potato chip" and "jiminy crickets" escaping his mouth with equal frequency as did complex explanations of Reformation-era politics and Greek mythology.

Unbeknownst to most, *The Arvid*'s captain was also its former owner – gained through inheritance and promptly sold to avoid the responsibility, notoriety, and lifestyle that came with owning a yacht. Ship was also keen to avoid any connection to the money he made from selling the boat to the Wilsons and kept the sizable amount of cash in a restricted trust. "In case I ever need it for doctors or what not," he had explained to Tom on their last cruise. "Or by some sick twist of fate I have a kid show up. Need ta give 'em a solid education, yah? The rest of it's on their own. But da schooling? That'd be on me."

"Why don't you want the money?" Tom asked.

"Les jus say I've seen what it does to ya, yah?" The captain shook his head. "Makes sane people crazy an' crazy people insane. Besides, I know from whence that money came an' I don' want any part of it."

"But you're still here. You only sold it to me on condition that you could stay on as captain."

"Yah. True." He shrugged his shoulders under a white t-shirt that had seen better days. "I was messed up when I finished school. All da money, all da connections, everythin' a kid could want or need . . . 'cept a sense of purpose an' belonging. So I convinced my parents ta let me sail dis boat with Captain Bernard during my gap year. Some kids work for orphanages in Africa or build houses in Eastern Europe. I worked dis boat." Ship nodded and looked around. "Learnt her inside out. Sailed da whole Caribbean, it seemed. Bernard never let on that my family owned it. Not ta any of da charter groups. Jus said I was 'the new deckhand, and a lousy one at that'." Ship smiled at the memory. "Great man. Great captain." He leaned back in his chair and took a sip of water. "He died of lung cancer about eight years ago. Some nasty shit, that cancer. He never saw it comin'. But ever since that year, I knew who I was meant ta be. Da captain of dis boat. I found myself on da ocean, Mr. Wilson. Some men weren't meant ta live on dry ground."

Tom imagined that his captain's wealthy upbringing was one reason the two men got along so well together. Whereas some workers could have trouble relating to the Wilsons' lifestyle and bristle at their success, Ship had no such problem. *Because he once had all of this himself,* Tom thought as he dropped his bags in the master stateroom before returning outside to the deck.

Noticing that the running lights were turned on to welcome them, Tom smiled. *Ryan will love that,* he thought. His teenage son's favorite part about the whole boat seemed to be the neon lights placed right above the waterline.

"Oooh, sweet!" the boy commented as if on cue. "Thanks for turning on the lights, Ship!" he added, walking across the gangplank onto *The Arvid.*

"You're welcome, Master Ryan," the captain replied.

Tom shook his head. "Every time we come down here, I have to spend the first half of the cruise convincing you to call me Tom and not to call my kids 'master' and 'miss'. Can we skip ahead to the part where you use our actual names?"

"Yes sir, if ya wish, Mr. Wilson," Ship replied with a wink and a smile.

"The lights really are awesome, even in the daytime," Ryan said, leaning over the rail to look down at them. "Check out how it reflects off the water. So sick."

"Who's sick?" asked Tom.

Ryan laughed. "Nobody. I said the lights look sick. Sick is good, Dad."

"If you say so."

"It makes about as much sense as 'groovy' or 'far out'," Ryan countered.

"You've got a point there," Tom said with a laugh. "Although, when I was your age I would've said the lights looked 'boss' or 'bitchin', not 'groovy'."

"Bitchin'?"

"Yeah," Tom said, nodding his head as he walked over to the wet bar and pulled out a bottle of scotch. Pouring himself a glass, he said: "your grandmother hated it. I think she almost fainted the first time she heard me say it."

Now it was Ryan's turn to laugh. After a minute, his

smile faded. "What was she like? Grandma, I mean. I never met her."

Tom leaned back against the bar and let out a deep sigh. "Serious. Very proper. There was a way things were done and she wouldn't hear any arguments to the contrary. That's how she showed you that she cared," he explained. "If you weren't important to her, she'd let you do what you wanted and dress how you wanted and say things like 'bitchin'. If you became a social pariah then who cares, right? No skin off her nose. But she wouldn't let that happen to the people she loved, so she made us follow the rules."

He took a sip of whisky and swirled the glass around in his hand. "New York society hasn't changed much since then, when you think about it. That's why your mom gives you grief for what you wear and how you talk. Because she loves you."

SIX

Later that night, after everyone unpacked and ate dinner al fresco on the boat, the six oldest members of the family gathered in the living room for the short walk from the marina to the Atlantis hotel casino.

"What am I supposed to do while you all get to gamble?" asked Ryan, still too young to join them.

Tripp shrugged his shoulders and ruffled his kid brother's hair. "What teenagers normally do – put on headphones and lock themselves in their room, playing video games and hating the world."

Ryan pulled away from his brother's reach and glared at him. "Screw you, man."

Tripp's eyes widened in mock surprise and he laughed. "Feisty little thing, aren't you?"

Ryan stood up from his chair and stepped toward his older brother. At almost six feet tall and still growing, he already towered over Tripp.

The elder Wilson son laughed again but also took a step backward. "Okay, okay, maybe not so little." He grinned. "Enjoy the quiet while we're gone. There certainly won't be any once we set sail."

****

After a couple of hands of blackjack and a round at the craps table, Tom cashed in his chips.

"Finished already?" asked MaryJo.

"I feel bad leaving Ryan there by himself. Figured I'd go play poker with him instead."

Mrs. Wilson smiled. "He'll love that. I'll come too."

Tom invited the rest of their group to join them, and Kay and Anya took him up on the offer. Tripp and Luke stayed behind.

Strolling past the rows of shops and restaurants that lined the walk between the hotel and the marina, Kay sighed and looked back toward the casino. "I wish Luke would've come with us," she whispered to Anya. "Dad will waive off any losses on the boat . . . I'm afraid the casino won't be as forgiving."

"Are you two in trouble?" Anya asked.

Kay, realizing what she said, straightened up tall and shook her head. "No, no, we're fine. Forget what I said. We're fine."

SEVEN

As was customary, *The Arvid* set sail early the next morning in order to beat the cruise ship traffic in and around Nassau.

After navigating the buoys and boats to reach the open sea, Captain Jones began a check of the yacht to ensure that nothing fell, broke, or jarred loose while leaving the harbor.

Breathing in the crisp sea air, Ship smiled. *There's a reason they call it Paradise Island*, he thought. The sky was a rich royal blue, dotted with fluffy clouds of white and the occasional seagull swooping down to hunt for fish in the crystal clear water below. *The Arvid*'s clean lines and powerful motor sliced through the Caribbean like butter. Ship lifted his face up toward the sun, soaking in the light that shined like rays of hope from Heaven and glistened on the water to create the illusion of millions of tiny diamonds dancing on the peaks of the gently rolling waves.

As he walked the length of the third and second decks, the captain noted that the rest of the yacht's passengers were still asleep. *As well they should be at 5:30 in the morning*, he thought. Ship smiled. It was his favorite time of day. No guests demanding this, that, or the other; no paths to chart or crew meetings to hold; no screaming toddlers or moody chefs to manage. *Jus me an' da sea*, he thought. *Perfection.*

When he reached the top deck, Ship realized that he wasn't the only one awake on *The Arvid*. Beside the table, seated in a chair, was Tom Wilson. The yacht's owner had his head in his hands and was rocking back and forth to a rhythm only he could hear.

Strange, Ship thought, but he didn't interrupt his boss. Jones' English desire for privacy mixed with his Caribbean free spirit to produce the perfect captain for the rich and famous: one who couldn't care less about their private lives.

Ship finished his check of the boat and then went to the

bridge, his command post located in the small covered portion of the top deck. All of the guests and crew knew that, if in doubt, the captain could be found there during most of the daylight hours.

A few minutes later, he felt a presence behind him. Turning around, Ship saw Mr. Wilson standing in the doorway.

"I thought I was the only one awake."

"So did I."

"I, umm, I saw you watching me out there," Tom said with a sheepish tone to his voice.

"None of my business, sir."

"I was praying. I like to get up in the mornings while it's still quiet and do my praying then."

"Like I said, none of my business." The captain paused. "But good for you, sir. I think that's great."

"Yeah?" Tom sighed. "I'm afraid my family wouldn't think so."

"They don' know about it? The prayin' an' all that?"

"No. I haven't gotten up the courage to tell them. If I tell them I've started praying every day and going to church, they'll want to know why. And that's an answer I can't give."

"I get it," Ship said with a nod. "We all have stuff we keep ta ourselves. As long as it's not hurtin' anybody, right?" He paused. "Maybe that's why I love bein' at sea. I keep a little plaque in my room," he said, gesturing below deck toward the staff quarters. "It's a quote by Robin Lee Graham, a guy who did a solo sail 'round da world when he was a teenager. He says that 'at sea, I learned how little a person needs, not how much.' I love that," the captain commented. "In a world obsessed with gettin' more an' more stuff, bigger an' shinier an' newer, the sea doesn't care. It doesn't let you care. It's jus' man an' beast out here."

"You do realize you're saying all of this while sitting on the bridge of an $8 million yacht?"

"Don' ruin my story with facts," Ship said with a smile. "But really," he added, "even on these megayachts, when push comes ta shove, it's jus' you an' da waves. I love that."

EIGHT

Four hours later, *The Arvid* was bustling with activity. Breakfast had come and gone. Tom and MaryJo were layout out on the top deck, their two little granddaughters were settled onto the living room couch watching cartoons, and all but one of the middle generation of Wilsons were seated around the dining room table playing Spades.

"I want to let my food settle first before I put on my bathing suit," Kay commented. "There's nothing worse than feeling bloated while wearing a bikini."

Anya looked over at her rail-thin sister-in-law and rolled her eyes. "You? Give me a break. Imagine how I feel with a whole other person riding around in my stomach."

"I can imagine. I've done it twice. And that baby is the size of a lime right now. I can't even tell you're pregnant."

"Are we going to talk babies or are we going to play cards?" asked Luke.

"Cards."

"Boys versus girls," Tripp suggested. "Luke and me against the wives."

All four turned to look as Ryan walked by with a tennis racket in his hand.

"What are you gonna do?" his sister asked. "Hit balls out into the water?"

"Not balls. The cook, Serena, gave me some block ice cubes. I'm going to work on my serve."

"Nah, don't do that," said Tripp. "Come join us."

"No thanks. Besides, Spades is a four-person game."

"Congrats on making Varsity," Luke said. "I don't think I've seen you since Kay told me the news."

The teenager smiled. "Thanks. I'm really excited."

"I bet Dad is too," Kay added. "He loved it when I played field hockey in school. He would show up for random games unannounced and be the most obnoxious fan in the stands. It embarrassed the crap out of me, but I always knew when he was there. Of course, Mom hated me playing field hockey," she said. "'All that bending over and it's so violent . . . ten years of dance lessons down the drain'," Kay said, imitating her mother's voice.

Ryan looked at his sister with a mixture of surprise and pain in his eyes. "Dad's never come to my tennis matches."

"Well, that's probably because your school is like four hours away."

"And Miss Porter's is super close? It's near Hartford!"

Tripp jumped into the fray between his siblings, trying to keep it from escalating and drawing their parents' attention from the top deck.

"Dad didn't start going to Kay's field hockey games until she made Varsity," Tripp explained. "You were on the JV tennis team this past year. Besides," he said, "every time you've had a tournament in the city, Dad's been there."

Ryan paused. "Yeah, that's true. And I didn't know it was only your Varsity games, Kay."

She nodded her head, feeling bad about hurting her little brother's feelings. "I'm sure that's it. I bet he's planning to surprise you at a match next year."

"In that case, I better go work on my serve," Ryan replied, twirling his racket in his hand as he left.

****

Up top, Ryan found both of his parents asleep in the sun. Not wanting to wake them up with the noise of tennis practice, he put his racket down on the table and walked into the bridge.

Technically an area reserved for the crew, Ryan knew that the captain wouldn't mind his visit.

"Hey Ship. Whatcha doin'?"

"Good mornin', Master Ryan. I'm lookin' at da wind forecasts for our trip."

29

"This isn't a sailboat. Why do you need to pay attention to the wind?"

"*Da Arvid*'s a big, beautiful, powerful machine, young sir, but we're still at da mercy of da seas out here. Never forget that. Gotta pay attention ta everythin'."

"Where'd the boat get its name?" Ryan asked.

"Her name."

"Huh?"

"Where'd da boat get *her* name," Ship corrected. "Boats are girls."

Ryan rolled his eyes. "Okay, where'd she get her name?"

"Somethin' ta do with da old owner," Ship replied with a shrug of his shoulders, hiding the fact that he knew exactly why the boat had that name. "Been that way as long as I've known her." The captain paused. "I 'member asking your dad when he bought her if he wanted ta change da name. He said no, so she stayed *Da Arvid*."

Ship aimed his patented lazy smile in the direction of the youngest Wilson. "There's da summer research project ya said ya were lookin' for earlier. Find out da hist'ry of your family's yacht."

The teenager nodded his head. "Yeah, that could actually be kinda cool. Thanks Ship!" Ryan bounded out of the bridge and downstairs toward his stateroom to get his laptop.

After the boy left, Captain Jones laughed. *Attention span of a fruit fly, that one.* "Good kid, though," he added aloud. "Good kid."

NINE

With morning naps complete and the sun shining brilliantly in the afternoon sky, Ship threw down anchor off the coast of an uninhabited island so that everyone could swim.

"Don't forget sunscreen!" MaryJo called out. "I don't want a boat full of lobsters!"

"A plate full of lobster would be nice," Tripp replied.

MaryJo swatted her son with her towel. "You know what I mean. And we're having lobster the last night of the cruise . . . but only if you behave and put on sunscreen."

Tripp smiled. "Excellent. Deal."

He then dove head first into the water, splashing everyone around him. Ryan returned the favor, and soon an all-out water war erupted off the starboard side of the yacht.

Tom watched from the top deck, laughing at the spectacle below.

When peace was declared, Kay and Anya went back to floating on their rafts while Tripp, Luke, and Ryan swam around the back of the boat to unhook the two jet skis stored underneath.

"Be careful with swimmers in the water," Tom warned.

"We will be, Dad. Don't worry."

"Did you spray with sunscreen?" asked MaryJo as she walked over to sit beside her husband.

"Yes. Twice. You've asked me twice as well."

"Sorry, I'm just trying to make sure." Changing subjects, she said: "it was nice to see Ryan talking to Ship earlier this morning. Like father like son, hanging around the captain."

Tom smiled and took a sip from his omnipresent glass of whisky. "I do love this boat, that's for sure. And I love that boy. He's my only chance for a little excitement in this family. I hope he marries his secretary. Or a cocktail waitress. Something fun."

"I think that's enough, Thomas," his wife scolded, reaching for his glass.

Anticipating the move, he switched the two fingers worth of scotch to his other hand and held it away from his body.

"Not enough," he replied. "'Tis never enough," the businessman said, a slur beginning to round off his words. "I ammmmm fiiiiiinnneee."

"Really, honey. Why don't you take a day off? Give your liver a break?"

"I don't need a babysitter."

Tom took another long sip of his drink and slammed his hand down on the table, shattering the glass. Whisky and blood spilled everywhere.

"Oh my God," MaryJo exclaimed. "Grab a towel," she ordered, before realizing there was no one else around them. "Kids! Get up here! Your dad cut his hand!"

"I ammmmm fiiiiiinnneee," Tom repeated as he used his good hand to push up out of his chair. The sixty-four year old raised his eyebrows, closed his eyes, and swayed back and forth before he plopped back down in his chair. "Rough seasss today."

"That's one word for it," the first mate, Marcelo, muttered under his breath as he hurried over with a towel and a First Aid kit.

"Here, I'll do it," said Ship, having heard the commotion and emerged from the bridge. "I'm afraid you'll have ta wait 'til we get ta Staniel Cay before ya can get proper treatment at a clinic, Mr. Wilson. But we can make do for now.

"The good thing is," the captain added, "ya have enough whisky in ya ta numb da pain when I start ta stitch ya up."

TEN

The afternoon and evening passed by uneventfully. An injured Thomas borrowed Ryan's headphones to watch a movie on his iPad, and the rest of the family tip-toed around their patriarch to avoid poking the bear.

"Animals lash out when they're injured and vulnerable," Kay whispered.

"He's a person, not a caged lion," Tripp replied.

"The principle still applies."

Looking around the main level of the yacht, Tripp saw that his wife and Luke were preoccupied with their cell phones. Madison and Harper had been put to bed an hour earlier. "You think now's a good time?" he asked.

"Yeah," said Kay. "Ryan, c'mon. We're doing it now."

****

"Hey Mom?" Kay said, peeking her head around the corner of MaryJo's bedroom.

"Yes honey?" she replied, looking in the mirror at the reflection of her daughter behind her.

"Can we talk to you for a minute?"

"We?" MaryJo turned and saw that Tripp and Ryan had joined their sister in the doorway. "Umm, sure, come on in."

The three Wilson children walked into the master stateroom and Ryan closed the door behind them.

"What's going on?"

The siblings glanced back and forth between each other.

"Don't look at me," said Ryan, shoving his hands in his pockets.

"You do it," Kay said, nudging Tripp with her elbow. "You're the oldest."

Tripp sighed. "The thing is, Mom . . . well, we're worried about Dad."

MaryJo sat down on the edge of her bed and motioned for her kids to join her. "Worried about him how?"

"He's never drank as much alcohol as he does now," Ryan blurted out. "He's like a different person."

"Ryan's right," Kay said. "I've never seen Dad like this before. What's going on?"

MaryJo sighed and stress lines wrinkled her face. "I honestly don't know. It started a couple of months ago. I've asked him and he says he's fine and to stop worrying, but . . ."

"Is the business okay?" Kay asked, looking at Tripp.

"As far as I know."

"I talked to Charles," said MaryJo, referencing her husband's business partner. "I thought it might be something work-related, but he told me things have never been better."

"So Dad's drinking himself stupid and we have no idea why," Ryan concluded.

"What if he's sick?" Kay suggested, her voice at a whisper.

Silence filled the room.

After a minute, their mom spoke. "I can't force his doctors to tell us something that your father doesn't want us to know."

"So he is sick?"

MaryJo shrugged her shoulders. "I don't know."

Kay stood up from the bed and put her hands on her hips. "We need to stage an intervention. Get all of us and Dad in a room and not let him leave until he's told us the truth and we have a plan to fix it."

Mrs. Wilson smiled. *She's so much like her father. See the problem and attack it head on.*

Tripp huffed in disapproval. "Good luck with that one."

And he's me, she thought. *Cynical and hesitant to a fault.*

Kay glared at her brother.

"Don't look at me like that," he shot back. "I'm with

Dad every day at work. I've seen the full effect of the new him. There's no way he agrees to a meeting."

"That's why it's called an *intervention*. He's not supposed to be happy about it."

"On the boat," Ryan suggested. "The last night of the cruise. That way he'll have nowhere to run."

"Except overboard."

"Thomas Arthur Wilson," MaryJo snapped. "That's enough."

"Sorry, sorry. Okay, I'm in. We'll confront him on the last night – that way we don't ruin the whole trip for everybody."

ELEVEN

The next morning, a sober and embarrassed Tom sought out the peace and quiet of *The Arvid*'s secret patio: a five-by-five foot retractable deck that jutted out the starboard bow of the yacht and was only accessible from inside the master suite.

"I guess I've had better days, haven't I?" Tom said aloud in prayer. "Father Gerry definitely wouldn't approve of how I acted yesterday." He sighed. "*I* don't approve of how I acted yesterday."

Tom rubbed his hands over his face and looked up at the sky.

"I know I must seem like a selfish bastard for only ever talking about myself. But God, I can't see past where I am right now. Gerry's always talking about forgiveness – how I need to ask You for forgiveness and eventually ask my family for forgiveness." Tom scoffed. "The family one is never going to happen. I'm serious here, God. How can I legitimately expect other people – even You – to forgive me if I can't forgive myself?"

"Here you are," MaryJo said as she stepped out of the master bedroom onto the patio. "Are you on the phone? Who were you talking to?"

"What? Oh, nobody. Talking some things through with myself."

"I understand," MaryJo said as she sat down in the patio's second lounge chair. "It's amazing how crowded a 121-foot yacht can feel."

"Were they this much noise when they were younger?"

"Who, the kids?" MaryJo shrugged. "Probably. But with Luke and Anya here it's five, not three. Plus the girls and the crew."

"You're right," Tom said with a nod. "Even so, it's hard to remember a time when I was there when they were

36

younger. Except for holidays and vacations. I always got home so late from the office that Tripp and Kay were already asleep. Left before they woke up for school."

"Where's this coming from?"

"I don't know. Maybe it's the whole grandfather thing hitting me. A new generation of Wilsons coming along to show me how much I missed with the last one."

MaryJo stood up from her chair and stepped in front of her husband. Bending down, she rested her hands on either side of his face.

"You are a good father. A good provider. The kids know how hard you work so we can all enjoy the life and the things we have." She leaned forward and softly kissed him. "Besides, it's not too late. Quit hiding out here and get in there with all of the noise. Don't miss this part of their lives because you're too hung up about missing the first part."

Tom sighed and nodded his head. "You're right." Pushing himself up from his chair, he said, "I really am looking forward to being a grandfather for a third time. Imagine if it's a boy. Thomas Wilson IV . . ."

MaryJo laughed. "I, for one, hope it's a girl. She'll have you wrapped around her little finger in no time, Gramps, just like Harper and Maddie."

"Watch it, *MamaJo*. Those are my little princesses you're talking about."

Laughter filled the master stateroom as Mr. and Mrs. Wilson made their way inside and toward the happy sounds of their family gathered around the breakfast table.

As they walked, Tom's smile remained but his thoughts returned to his unfinished prayers from a few minutes earlier. *Fake it 'til you make it, Tommy. Fake it 'til you make it.*

TWELVE

"I enjoyed these cruises more before we had WiFi," Tom said to himself a few minutes later, looking over at the table where each person had a cell phone or tablet in their hands.

"We can turn it off if ya want to, sir," Captain Jones replied.

Tom turned, startled. "Woah, didn't know you were standing there, Ship."

"Sorry, sir. But we can switch off da internet if ya want."

"They might riot."

"Mutiny is expressly forbidden on *Da Arvid*, Mr. Wilson."

Tom laughed. "Isn't mutiny forbidden on every ship?"

"Well . . . yah, I s'pose so."

"You know what? Switch it off. They'll survive. And I might actually get to see their faces and hear their voices for a change."

Ship smiled, agreeing with the decision. "Yes sir."

With their electronic distractions taken away, the yacht's guests did indeed start talking and enjoying each other's company.

Seated between his granddaughters on the living room couch, Tom smiled. *Now this is a vacation.*

At the other end of the sofa, the Wilson women were busy discussing Tripp and Anya's upcoming wedding anniversary.

"Six years at the end of September," Anya said. "It seems like only yesterday I was flying from Zurich to London and a handsome stranger sat down next to me."

Kay smiled. "I love how you two met. Luke and I are such a standard story: college sweethearts. To meet on a flight in Europe? That's so cool."

"How did you and Tom meet?" Anya asked MaryJo. "I don't think you ever told me."

"I was a senior at Ole Miss," MaryJo replied. As soon as she started talking about her college days, her Southern accent came roaring back to life.

"I didn't know you went to Old Miss," said Anya. "I always thought you went to school somewhere near New York."

"It's *Ole* Miss, not *Old* Miss," MaryJo corrected. "And no, I was raised in New York but Mother insisted that I go to college in the South. Mother fought Daddy on that one big time. He wanted me to go to one of the Seven Sisters – Radcliffe, Mount Holyoke, etc. – but Mother was adamant that I go to Ole Miss. Feminism was riding a high wave during that time, and Mother said that if I went to a northern college I'd turn into some 'raging liberal lesbian freak'."

Kay and Anya shook their heads.

"You can't say stuff like that, Mom."

"I didn't say it – your grandmother did. Over and over. So Daddy finally agreed to send me to Ole Miss for a 'proper lady's education'."

"Did you ever consider staying in the South?"

MaryJo nodded her head. "Very briefly, at the strong urging of my boyfriend at the time: Teddy Lindwood. Dr. Edward Lindwood now," she said. "We still exchange Christmas cards every year. Anyway, I loved Ole Miss and I loved Teddy, but I missed New York. The excitement, the culture, the energy. I'm glad I went to college in the South and have that connection to my mom and our shared history, but I'm a New Yorker. I think I always knew I'd end up back there."

"You said your mom wanted you to go to Ole Miss and your dad 'sent' you there," said Ryan, having joined the conversation. "Did you not get a vote?"

MaryJo laughed and shook her head. "Things were different back then. A lot of women still didn't even go to college, let alone get to decide where. Plus, as you know, he who pays the piper calls the tune. There are a lot of privileges associated with coming from money, but there are also a lot of strings."

"Where does Dad fit into all of this?"

"I met your father at a New Year's Eve party at his parents' house. I was headed into my final semester of college. Teddy and I had broken up the previous year after he graduated, and your dad was a fresh-faced analyst at his father's firm. We danced all evening, talked all night, and I told Mother the next morning that I'd met my future husband."

"Love at first sight?"

She nodded. "Pretty close. Of course, we found out a few months later that it was all a set-up. My mom and his mom arranged for us to both attend the party and be introduced. But by that time we were so happy together that we didn't care." MaryJo smiled. "It all worked out in the end."

"If given the chance, would you do it all over again?" asked Kay.

"Absolutely. In a heartbeat."

THIRTEEN

"I heard you talking about the party where we met," Tom said that night after another long, fun day at sea. "We were the 'it' couple in New York society that year. Our wedding was the hottest ticket in town. If they only knew how poor we were," he said with a laugh. "I was still an entry-level analyst and my dad refused to help us out. Do you remember that?" Tom asked. "Senior said he wanted us to learn what real struggle was."

MaryJo shook her head. "Nuh-uh. He thought I was a mix-breed because my mom was Southern. He made us live in that rat hole for a year to test our relationship."

"That's not true."

"It is true! He told me so while he and I were dancing at our wedding reception. He said, 'we'll see how much you really love my son when I take away all of his money'."

Tom looked at his wife in shock. "You never told me that before."

She shrugged her shoulders. "Going through all of that is what pushed you to go out on your own. To step out of Senior's shadow. Besides, it turned out okay in the end."

Tom grinned and looked around the stateroom of their yacht. "I think things are a little better than okay." He walked over to MaryJo and wrapped his arms around her waist. "Plus, that first apartment wasn't so bad."

"A fifth floor walkup with no air conditioning and a seven-block uphill hike to get to the subway?"

Tom pulled her closer. "At least it was downhill coming home, right? And those five flights of stairs did wonders for your ass."

MaryJo slapped her husband on the shoulder. "Thomas!"

"What? It did. I kinda liked those close quarters," he added with a lecherous grin. "Lots of quality time."

Mrs. Wilson tried to stifle a laugh. "Is that what the kids

41

are calling it these days?"

"Who the hell knows. Damn Millennials. They probably don't call it anything. I'm sure there's some combination of emojis that they FaceSnap to each other."

"FaceTime. Snapchat," MaryJo corrected.

"Whatever. More importantly, how would you like to get in a little quality time right now?"

MaryJo's smile faded and the playfulness left her eyes. She pulled out of Tom's embrace.

"I can't, honey. Not tonight."

"Not any night, at this rate."

She sighed. "Don't start with me."

"Start? I never get close to starting with you anymore. And I can't even remember the last time we got to the finish."

MaryJo rolled her eyes. "The answer is no." Turning on her heel, she stalked out of the bedroom.

Tom put his hands on his hips and let out a deep breath. Looking up at the ceiling, he said, "I'm trying, God. I'm really trying here. But that damn . . . sorry, dang woman isn't giving me anything to work with. A little help would be nice."

The businessman shook his head in frustration and walked across the room to his nightstand. Opening the drawer, he pulled out an empty glass and a bottle of whisky. Tom poured the glass half-full with 20-year Macallan before sitting down on the edge of the bed.

"What's the use, anyway?" he asked aloud. "I'm already damned to Hell. Making up with my wife isn't going to change that."

Tom downed the single malt scotch in one gulp and reached for the bottle to pour another. *The God of Abraham hasn't made me feel any better*, he thought, *but the god of Scotland sure will.*

FOURTEEN

The next day dawned bright and beautiful in the Bahamas, and Ship once again dropped anchor. From the back deck of the second level, Kay smiled as she watched her two daughters swim in the water with their grandparents.

MaryJo was holding Harper, with the fifteen month old covered head-to-toe in inflatable safety gear. Madison, on the other hand, was giggling and screaming with delight while 'Tom Tom' pretended to be a shark and grabbed her ankles from underneath the water.

"They're so happy," Kay commented.

"Hmm?"

"I said they're so happy."

"Who is?" Luke asked.

Kay sighed in disgust and reached over to lower her husband's cell phone from in front of his face. "Our daughters," she said, pointing out toward the water.

"Oh, yeah," he replied before returning his attention to his phone.

"I was thinking it'd be nice to have a third, don't you?"

Upon hearing that remark, Luke lowered his cell phone and turned to face his wife. "We can't afford a third kid, Katherine. We can barely afford the two we already have."

"Shhh," Kay whispered. "Everyone will hear you!"

"You know what? Maybe they should hear me," he said, standing up from his chair. "Maybe it'd be good for someone in this family to tell the truth for a change."

Luke stormed inside the boat in the direction of the kitchen.

Probably to find the liquor cabinet, Kay thought.

"Is everything okay, honey?" Tom asked, having overheard Luke's outburst.

"Yeah, Dad, no problem. Everything's fine."

43

FIFTEEN

The Wilsons had been cruising the Lower Bahamian Islands for ten years before they discovered the oasis of Staniel Cay. Located seventy-five miles southeast of Nassau in a chain called The Exumas, Staniel Cay Yacht Club was a beautiful boutique resort with fourteen bungalows, a restaurant, and a full-service marina. Each guest was assigned their own small boat for exploring the area, and one of the most popular activities was feeding breakfast scraps to the pigs who swam off the island's coast.

After Kay and Luke spent their honeymoon on Staniel and raved about it to their families, Tom and MaryJo decided to add the spot to their annual itinerary.

On the afternoon of the fourth day of their cruise, *The Arvid* moored in the waters off Staniel Cay and Marcelo ferried the Wilsons over to the island on the yacht's dinghy.

"Why little boat?" asked Madison as their inflatable rubber raft glided over The Exumas' calm waters.

"Our boat is too big to dock at the marina," her mom explained, "so we ride over in this little boat. After dinner, Marcelo will bring us back to *The Arvid*."

"Oh," the little girl replied, brushing a hand over her pink dress to remove the drops of seawater that sprayed up on her. Per her mom's instructions, Maddy held her shoes in her other hand. "You can put them on once we get there," Kay said. "We don't want to accidentally pop the boat."

There was little chance of the three and a half year old's sandals doing any damage to the sturdy, reinforced rubber of the dinghy, but Kay, Anya, and MaryJo's stiletto heels were another story.

With the women wearing a stunning array of Chanel, Temperley, and Alice & Olivia, and the men stepping out in Billy Reid, Yves Saint Laurent, and Hermès, the Wilson family were without a doubt the most fashionable guests at the Yacht Club that evening. *As we should be*, MaryJo thought.

While the rest of the party went straight to the dining room, Tom made a pit stop at the medical clinic to have the gash in his hand examined.

"How'd this happen?" the nurse-in-residence asked while cleaning and re-stitching the wound.

"Should've known better than to mix whisky and water," the patient replied with a grin.

"If I had a dollar for every time I've heard that one . . ."

"You'd own the island instead of working on it, right?"

"Exactly." The nurse wrapped gauze and medical tape around Tom's hand and leaned back on her stool. "All done. Stitches can come out in ten days. You'll need to keep this clean and dry until then. I know that can be difficult while you're on vacation in the Caribbean."

Tom shook his head. "No problem. Clean, dry, and stitches out in ten days. Got it. Thanks, doc."

She laughed. "I'm a nurse, but you're welcome. Have a good rest of your trip, Mr. Wilson."

Tom nodded and waved goodbye before walking the short distance between the medical hut and the main clubhouse to rejoin his family for dinner. Seated around a large table in the back of the room, the rest of the Wilsons were looking through the restaurant menu, complete with fresh food items flown in daily from the United States.

Madison and Harper quickly selected PB&J and macaroni and cheese before turning their attention to the coloring books Kay brought for them.

"The vegetable stir-fry looks amazing," said Anya, the only vegetarian in the group.

"Don't you need to eat, like, meat and stuff now that you're pregnant?" Ryan asked.

"No."

"What about like protein or whatever?"

"What about it? I get plenty of protein and other

45

nutrients from beans, peas, and soy products."

"Soy. Gross." Ryan made a gagging face.

"She doesn't have to eat meat if she doesn't want to," said Tom. Turning to face his daughter-in-law, he added: "do be sure to take care of yourself, though. You're eating for two now."

Anya nodded and pursed her lips together in a toothless smile. "I know. I will."

The rest of the family decided on a combination of lobster and the catch of the day, and MaryJo ordered her usual: duck confit.

"How's Daffy taste, Mom?"

Seven adults glared at Ryan, while Madison's face turned white and she looked at her grandmother with eyes as big as saucers. "You eat Daffy Duck?"

Ryan laughed at his joke, but the rest of the table jumped into damage control mode.

"No, no honey. I'm not eating Daffy," MaryJo promised.

"Daffy is safe," Kay added. "Nobody is eating Daffy."

Looking down at his plate, Ryan felt the heat of his father's glare. The teenager risked a glance toward the end of the table but immediately regretted it. Tom slowly shook his head back and forth, the ultimate disapproval, and to Ryan it felt worse than a punch in the gut.

Shit, he thought, regretting his Daffy the Duck remark more and more with each passing second. *The less Dad says, the madder he is.*

Turning to his niece, Ryan tried to minimize the amount of trouble he would be in later. "I'm sorry, Maddy. I was kidding. Grandma isn't eating Daffy. It was supposed to be a joke."

The little girl blinked at him through tears. "No funny."

The table went silent, and after a few seconds Tom started laughing. "She told you, buddy!"

The rest of the Wilson party joined in the laughter and Ryan breathed a sigh of relief. *Out of the woods . . . for now at least.*

****

The rest of the dinner passed without event, and, three hours after they arrived, the fashionable family boarded their plastic dinghy to return to the yacht. Much to everyone's relief, Tom stayed sober enough to board both the little and big boats under his own power.

A functionality which didn't last long.

"Come on, men," Tom said as he opened the doors of the dining room's liquor cabinet and grabbed two bottles of whisky.

"There's no law saying you have to drink every night of the trip," MaryJo commented.

"Sure there is. It's the custom of the sea."

"Umm, we learned about the custom of the sea in history class," Ryan said. "If that's what you're planning, count me out."

Tom laughed and wrapped an arm around his son's shoulders. "Oh come on, I'm sure you'd taste delicious!"

"Thomas!"

"I was kidding," he replied. "You should come, though, Ry."

"Drinking on the top deck?" asked MaryJo. "I don't think so."

"The boy's almost sixteen. He can handle it. What about you, Luke? Gonna finally join us?"

"Not tonight."

At that, the two and a half Wilson men climbed up the curved staircase and disappeared out of view.

"So much for not enabling him," said Kay. "Tripp – and now Ryan – go and join him."

"Maybe if they're with him he'll drink less," her mom replied.

One floor up, Tom showed no intention of a light

evening when he poured a glass full of scotch for himself and Tripp and a smaller one for Ryan.

"I'm not crazy," Mr. Wilson said with a shrug. "However, I was once a boarding school student myself and I seem to recall stashed bottles, breath mints, and air fresheners."

Ryan's face turned red and he looked down at the glass of alcohol in his hand. "I . . ."

"I wasn't trying to put you on the spot. Only saying that nobody's perfect." Tom sighed. "Especially your old man."

"We drank a couple of times freshman year," Ryan said, causing Tripp to raise his eyebrows in surprise.

Braver kid than I was at that age, owning up to it in front of Dad.

"I can't drink now that I made Varsity, though," Ryan continued. "Coach makes us take random drug tests, and the whole team signed a 'clean living' pledge."

Tom smiled and raised his glass in the direction of his youngest child. "That's what it's gonna take if you want to play at the next level," he said. "Dedication. Sacrifice. A lack of cruel comments in front of your nieces."

"I know." Ryan nodded his head. "I can do it. And sorry about the Daffy thing."

The Wilson men heard footsteps on the stairs and saw Ship emerge from below deck.

"Oh, sorry," he said. "I didn't realize anyone was still up here."

"No worries," Tom replied. "Would you like a drink?"

"Thank ya sir, but no. Only fools an' passengers drink at sea."

"I thought the drunken sea captain was the ultimate stereotype," said Tripp.

"Drunk on shore, sober at sea, sir," Ship replied, tipping his cap and disappearing back down the spiral staircase.

On the top deck, the three passengers burst out laughing.

"A toast to our sober captain," Tom said, raising his

glass.

"To the sober captain!"

SIXTEEN

The next morning, the sober captain woke up early and began his routine survey of the yacht. *She's a finely-tuned machine,* he told his crew repeatedly. *A million tiny parts workin' together ta make somethin' beautiful. But if one of those things breaks, it all breaks.*

Reaching the top deck, Ship was surprised to find it empty.

"I guess Mr. Wilson isn't prayin' this mornin'," he said. "Not surprisin' that he'd sleep in, given how much he had ta drink last night."

An hour and a half later, Marcelo entered the bridge. "You seen da boss dis mornin'?"

"No. Why?"

"Can't find him."

The captain stopped what he was doing and turned to face his first mate. "*You* can't find him or nobody can find him?"

"Nobody."

"You've checked da whole boat?"

Marcelo nodded. "Top ta bottom."

Ship grabbed the radio transmitter hanging on the wall.

"PAN PAN. This is Da Arvid Da Arvid Da Arvid. 174183. This is Da Arvid. 24°24'33.6" North by 76°16'47.7" West. Twelve nautical miles North-Northeast of Staniel Cay Yacht Club. Passenger is overboard an' missin'. Request immediate SAR. Passenger is white male, sixty-four, knows how ta swim. Unknown how long he's been missin'. Repeat: request immediate SAR. Over."

The radio crackled while Ship waited for a response.

"Go check da water. Check his stateroom. Hell, check inside da dinghy. Everywhere."

Marcelo nodded and ran out of the room.

"Arvid this is Bahamas Air Sea Rescue. We've received

your PAN. Maintain current position. U.S. Coast Guard is being notified. Search and rescue on its way. Over."

"Copy. Over an' out."

Ship pressed the radio back into the wall and hit full stop on the engines. *The Arvid* lurched forward in response to the brakes.

"Marcelo! Please tell me ya found him asleep inside da kitchen pantry!"

****

A helicopter from the U.S. Coast Guard's Search and Rescue Readiness Team arrived at *The Arvid* forty-five minutes after Ship's distress call, its familiar orange and white markings hovering over the yacht while the blades created a miniature hurricane in the water.

Two men climbed down a swinging ladder from the helicopter onto the top deck, and then the chopper disappeared again into the blue Caribbean sky.

"Where are they going?!" asked MaryJo. "We need them!"

"They're sweeping the immediate area, ma'am," replied the lieutenant in charge.

His petty officer nodded in agreement. "We're here to set up a base and learn more information about the disappearance. We'll then coordinate with other rescue groups in the area to set up a SAR plan of action."

"How long has he been missing?" the lieutenant asked.

"We're not sure exactly," Ship replied. "Every other mornin' of da cruise he's been up on da top deck at 5:30 when I make my rounds, but I figured he slept in dis mornin'."

"When was the last time anyone saw him?"

"I went to bed at 1am," said Tripp. "He was still awake then."

"Mom, did Dad ever come to bed?" Kay asked.

51

"I-I don't know," MaryJo stammered through her tears. "I wasn't f-feeling well so I t-took some Nyquil bef-f-fore I went to sleep."

The lieutenant looked at his watch. "It's eight o'clock now. That means the man – what's his name?"

"Tom. Tom Wilson."

"That means Mr. Wilson has been in the water anywhere from one to seven hours. And the yacht was cruising up until the point you noticed he was missing, correct?"

Ship nodded. "East-Northeast at ten knots."

The two Coasties shook their heads.

"That's a big area to search," said the petty officer.

"Let me make a call," added the lieutenant.

He returned a few minutes later. "I've notified the Coast Guard Liaison Officer in Nassau. He'll coordinate with the Royal Bahamas Defense Force and the Bahamas Air Sea Rescue Association. The good thing is there's no shortage of boats and planes in the islands. Everyone who can pitch in with the SAR effort will do so. Do you have a grid map?" he asked.

"In da bridge," Ship replied. "I'll go get it."

When Captain Jones returned with the map, the lieutenant spread it out on the kitchen table. "Alright, we're here right now. This," he said, drawing a fan behind the ship's current location, "is our search area. Based on the time frame when he could've gone overboard, we'll do what's called a ladder search, or 'creeping line'. We already have Jayhawk helicopters in the air with rescue swimmers on board and ready to go in if we spot him. Seaplanes, rescue boats, and volunteer passenger vessels will also help search the area for where he might've gone in or drifted to by now.

"Our mission is to prevent the loss of life in every situation," he added. "This one is no different. This is a search and rescue – an all-out effort to find Mr. Wilson and bring him back safely."

"What can we do?" asked Tripp.

"If the yacht has a smaller boat, you can take it out and assist in the search effort. Aside from that, there's really not much you can do. If you go out, though," the Coastie cautioned, "be careful and don't go too far. The last thing we need is more people lost at sea."

SEVENTEEN

Eleven hundred miles away in New York City, the police commissioner was holding his morning senior staff meeting. Derrick Clark believed in surrounding himself with the best people, giving them direction, and then trusting them to do their jobs. This morning's meeting fell into the 'direction' category. With nearly 50,000 employees and an annual budget just shy of $5 billion, Commissioner Clark knew how important it was to stay on message and keep a finger on the pulse of the department.

Strong leadership was a lesson he learned from his two life mentors: his grandfather (also a police officer) and his college football coach. Derrick was a star linebacker at Harvard, winning three League titles and twice earning All-Ivy honors.

Clark's wife, Cindy, was a former public schoolteacher who had to retire when he was made commissioner. He had explained the situation to his best friend and former Harvard roommate, Tom Wilson, after he was sworn in. "It's too dangerous for her and the kids, and way too expensive to run a separate security detail for her. She hates me for it." Derrick flashed a crooked smile. "Truth be told, she's been talking about retiring for several years. I think what she resents is that it wasn't her choice."

Derrick and Cindy's two children, a daughter and a son, were both grown and lived out of state.

Sitting at the head of the conference table, Clark looked every inch of the powerful New Yorker he had become. Power suit, power tie, power haircut. The only thing that separated Derrick from the bankers on Wall Street was the quality of the fabric. *I learned that quickly at Harvard*, he thought, adjusting his tie. *Even though they said there was no official school uniform, there was absolutely an unofficial one. Just like in New York's upper echelon. I can't afford*

54

those same brands, but I can at least look close enough.

"Excuse me, Commissioner? You have a phone call."

His longtime assistant, Stephanie, stuck her head around the door.

"We'll be finished here soon," he replied. "Take a message."

Ten minutes later, Stephanie was waiting outside the conference room door. "The call was from Tripp Wilson, sir."

"You mean Tom."

"No sir, from his son, Tripp."

"What'd he want? I thought they were all in the Bahamas this week."

"They are, sir." His assistant sighed, worry lines creasing her brow. "Tom Wilson is missing."

Commissioner Clark stopped in the middle of the hallway.

"What?"

"Mr. Wilson, the younger, said that when they all woke up this morning his father wasn't on the boat. They've contacted the Coast Guard, but he said he was calling you in case you knew anyone who could make it a higher priority."

Derrick ran his hand over his face and back through his hair. "Oh my God. Did he – did he leave a number? C-can I call him back?"

Wow, Stephanie thought. *I've never seen him like this.* Nine years as Clark's executive assistant had exposed the woman to a host of highs and lows, triumphs and tragedies, but she'd never seen her boss as upset as he was now. She nodded her head in response to his question. "The connection was spotty but he said you could try calling this number."

Stephanie handed him a piece of paper. "That's Tripp's cell phone. He said not to call the boat directly because they need to keep the line clear for the search and rescue teams."

Three calls to Tripp's phone went unanswered.

"He's probably out searching," Stephanie suggested.

"Yeah, you're right."

Derrick had MaryJo's number in his contacts and tried her next.

No answer.

"Shit – doesn't anyone pick up the phone?!"

He dialed a third number.

"Cindy, it's me. Listen. I had a call from Tripp Wilson. Tom's missing. . . . Yes, in the Bahamas. . . . I don't know, apparently he wasn't on the boat when everyone woke up this morning. I've got another meeting in five minutes, but will you try calling MaryJo? Keep trying, and let me know if you get through. . . . Okay. Love you too."

The commissioner slid his cell phone into the side pocket of his jacket.

"I want constant updates on this," he told his assistant. "I don't care if I'm in a meeting. Constant updates."

"Yes sir."

****

In the Bahamas, Tripp, Marcelo, and Luke all climbed into the inflatable, eleven-foot dinghy that usually served to ferry the family from *The Arvid* to smaller marinas.

I can't believe it, Tripp thought, sitting down at the front of the boat and looking out into the water through binoculars. *Dad and I were on this raft twelve hours ago coming back from dinner. Now I'm using it to look for him in the ocean. Because he's missing.*

"What was he wearin' da last time ya saw him?" asked Marcelo, yelling over the sound of the engine chopping through the sea.

"Same thing he wore to dinner. Khaki slacks and a navy blue golf shirt."

The first mate nodded and resumed scanning the water.

"See anything?" Luke asked.

"Nothing."

56

For three hours, until they almost ran out of gas, Tom Wilson's son, son-in-law, and first mate searched the Caribbean for him. The dinghy hummed back and forth over the water, with the occasional dolphin or large fish jumping up and giving the men hope. But by the time they rushed over to the spot, the wildlife was gone and so was their chance of finding Tom.

Weary and sun-baked, the men returned to *The Arvid* empty-handed.

"I'm sorry, Mom," Tripp said, wrapping his arms around MaryJo. "We'll refuel and go out again. We're going to find him. We won't stop until we find him."

EIGHTEEN

That evening in New York, police detective Dennis Van Hatcher threw his keys on the kitchen counter of his prewar Brooklyn apartment and walked to the refrigerator. After another long day at work, this one involving a domestic dispute and a potential money laundering ring, the forty-four year old NYPD veteran was looking forward to a cold beer, a quiet dinner, and a Yankees game on TV.

A NYC native, Dennis was of average height and slender-to-average build, depending on his donuts-to-situps ratio that particular month. July was bathing suit season, so the divorcée with a penchant for dating younger women was in his best shape of the year.

Nothing, Dennis thought, staring into the near-empty fridge. Over a decade after his divorce, he still lived like a twenty-something bachelor. Opening the freezer, Dennis spotted a frozen chicken pot pie. *That'll do.*

Ten minutes later, Detective Van Hatcher had changed from his work suit into gym shorts and a t-shirt. Sitting down on the couch, he put the pot pie in his lap and rested his beer bottle against him on the sofa. He glanced at the clock on the wall. *Seven pm. The game doesn't start until 7:30*, he thought. "Might as well catch a little local news, right buddy?" Dennis said, talking to the cat who emerged from the bedroom and jumped up to join his owner on the couch.

Murphy was a gorgeous, fluffy Maine Coon with a white chest, black and brown stripes on his body, and white stockings on his feet. Dennis planned on naming him Boots because of his markings, but decided on Murphy as an ode to his mother's Irish roots.

"I bet if I'd named you Boots you wouldn't try to steal my food," he said, holding his dinner up high in the air while Murphy rubbed himself against the detective's side.

"Hello to you too, Murph. Yes, I missed you too. But

you're still not getting any of my dinner."

Murphy looked up at his owner, issued a curt "meow" in protest, and stalked into the kitchen.

Dennis laughed. "Crazy cat."

Flipping on the television, he turned to the local news station right as it was finishing the weather forecast.

"Record heat expected to continue through the week and into the weekend, so be sure to stay hydrated and indoors whenever possible. Some much-needed rain will arrive early next week and bring cooler temperatures with it." The meteorologist smiled. "Back to you, Fred."

"Thanks Hannah," the news anchor replied. "Turning now to a story that is grabbing headlines here and around the world. NYC native and business tycoon Tom Wilson has been reported missing while vacationing with his family in the Bahamas."

Dennis looked up from his dinner to pay closer attention to the television.

"For more on this story, we'll go to Anthony Quinn on the Upper East Side. Anthony?"

"Thanks Fred," the reporter said. "I'm here tonight outside the home where the missing millionaire, Thomas Wilson II, lives with his wife and teenage son. A giant figure on Wall Street and in New York's high society, Mr. Wilson reportedly went missing overnight from his family's yacht. The Coast Guard and local Bahamian search and rescue crews are working overtime trying to find the man. Wilson's wife, children, and grandchildren were all on the boat with him at the time of his disappearance," the reporter added. "As you can imagine, his friends and business associates here in the city are shocked by the news. That's an angle I'm working on for the eleven o'clock hour. Back you to in the studio."

Dennis tuned out the rest of the news broadcast as he thought about the missing man. "Tom Wilson," he said in barely more than a whisper. "Shit. I can't even imagine what the commissioner is like right now."

The twenty-two year veteran (and everyone else in the NYPD) knew that Commissioner Clark and Tom Wilson were best friends. *Hell, I think they were in each other's weddings*, thought Dennis.

He groaned aloud. "That means he's gonna be a living terror at our meeting tomorrow. Shit."

As a detective first-grade with a well-deserved reputation for cracking the cases that no one else could, Van Hatcher had earned himself a seat at the table for the commissioner's monthly gathering of precinct leaders. *And the next one is tomorrow. Of course.*

NINETEEN

Tom Wilson's body was found at 6:45am the next morning, nearly twenty-four hours after he was reported missing.

"Who found him?" asked the Coast Guard lieutenant spearheading the search.

"A fisherman. Washed up on the southern end of Eleuthera."

The lieutenant and Tripp rode in a Bahamian military helicopter from *The Arvid* to the small island to identify the body.

"In here," the local constable said. "We don' have a morgue on da island, so we're usin' an empty meat freezer."

Tripp felt his breakfast lurch in his stomach.

The constable lifted a white sheet to reveal the dead man's face.

Tripp covered his mouth with his hand and lunged toward a garbage can in the corner.

With the contents of his stomach resting at the bottom of the trash, Tripp wiped his mouth against his sleeve and nodded his head. "That's him."

"You sure?"

"Yeah."

"That's all we needed from you. Thank you, Mr. Wilson."

"Why . . . why does he look like that?"

"Like what?" asked the policeman.

"Bloated and puffy."

The Coast Guard officer stepped forward to explain. "When a person drowns or a body enters the water, the cadaver will float for a little while. Once the air in the lungs is replaced by water, though, the body will sink. Eventually, bacteria in the gut and chest cavity produce gas, and the body will inflate and rise to the surface like a balloon."

"So that's why he's all puffy? Gases and stuff?"

"Yes sir. It's very common in situations like this."

"Can you tell –" Tripp paused. "Can you tell what killed him?"

Both officials shook their heads.

"We'll have to wait for the autopsy."

****

One Police Plaza, or '1PP' for short, was the headquarters for the New York City Police Department. Located on Park Row near City Hall in Manhattan, 1PP was a large, brown, fortress-like building with windows lining all but the top of the fifteen-story box-shaped edifice.

Once a month, the captains from all seventy-six NYPD precincts, as well as select other members of the department, crowded into a theater for a status meeting with the commissioner.

Halfway through a presentation about a successful drug ring bust, Commissioner Clark's assistant walked up and passed him a note.

MaryJo Wilson is on the phone.

Clark stood up and followed Stephanie backstage.

"MaryJo," Derrick said when he picked up the line. "Is there any news?"

"They found him."

"Is he –"

Derrick heard sobbing on the other end of the phone before it went silent. A few seconds later, Kay picked up.

"Hi Mr. Derrick," she said, using the name she'd called him since she was a little girl.

"Hi sweetheart. He's dead?"

"Yeah. They found him on the beach of an island nearby."

Derrick placed the receiver on his shoulder and closed his eyes. *Shit.* Tears threatened to overrun New York's top cop.

"Is there anything I can do?" he asked. "Anything at all?"

"Hold on, Mom wants to talk to you again."

"The police here are crap," MaryJo said, anger replacing her earlier sadness.

"I know they're probably not what you're used to, but I don't have any reason to doubt the professionalism of the Bahamian police."

"They're crap," she repeated. "They kept him in a damn meat freezer. A meat freezer. Like he's tomorrow night's dinner."

"What can I do, MaryJo?"

"He's a New Yorker. Can't you investigate what happened?"

Derrick sighed into the phone. "It's not my jurisdiction, MaryJo. There's not much I can do without their agreement, but I'll call down there and try to see what's going on."

"Thanks. You're a great friend." MaryJo paused and sniffed back fresh tears. "Thomas loved you like a brother. You know that, right?"

"I do. It was mutual."

TWENTY

Later that afternoon, Dennis Van Hatcher and his partner, Detective Vanessa Smith, were summoned to 1PP from their office at the 5th Precinct.

As a Detective First Grade, Van Hatcher was an elite, experienced investigator with the gold badge to prove it. He wore the shield on his left hip and his service weapon on the right, both half-concealed beneath a fitted black suit jacket.

His partner was eleven years younger and eleven years less experienced. Vanessa Smith, the daughter of Haitian immigrants, wore her badge on a chain around her neck. Five foot six and curvy, she preferred slacks, button-down shirts, and a thin rain jacket with NYPD printed on the back in block letters.

"Just in case the badge and gun didn't announce your presence loudly enough?" Dennis asked after they passed through security to enter police headquarters.

"I'm a cop. My husband's a teacher. We pay rent through the nose and have student loan debt coming out our eyeballs. I'll take whatever free clothes I can get." She reached out and pressed the button for the elevator. "Besides, you're not much better, Mr. I'm-Too-Cool-To-Wear-A-Tie."

Dennis laughed. "Okay, okay. Touché. But . . . maybe it wouldn't kill you to wear a different color shirt every now and then? I'm sure Roman would appreciate it."

Ignoring the comment about her husband, Vanessa said: "speaking of killing people, are we really being assigned the Tom Wilson case?"

"Who told you that?"

"Well, actually what I heard was that you were getting put on the case, but since I was called over to 1PP with you, I figured maybe we both were."

Dennis shrugged his shoulders. "Dunno. I guess we'll find out soon enough."

****

A courtesy call to the commissioner of the Royal Bahamas Police Force had revealed that Mrs. Wilson's 'crap' description was an exaggeration – *if not flat out wrong*, Derrick Clark thought while waiting for the detectives to arrive.

The meat freezer part was true, but only because the small island where the body was found didn't have a proper morgue. As soon as transport could be arranged, Tom Wilson's corpse was flown to Nassau. *The Arvid* was also placed under police control as a potential crime scene.

They've done everything right, it seems.

A knock on the door was followed by the entrance of Detectives Van Hatcher and Smith.

"Have a seat," the commissioner said, gesturing toward the two chairs opposite his desk. "Thanks for coming in. My assistant tells me that word has gotten out about Tom Wilson's death."

"I think the whole world knows about it, sir," Dennis replied. He had known Commissioner Clark for over twenty years and felt comfortable expressing his opinion in front of him.

"I meant word has gotten around that I want you to investigate it. Which is correct – I do."

"Shouldn't what's-his-face up in the 19th take this?" Dennis asked. "That's where the potential vic lived."

Commissioner Clark shook his head. "No. Townsend is a fine detective, but I don't want him on it."

"But –"

"But nothing. Tom Wilson was my best friend. I don't want some Third-Degree, 'find my Pomeranian', shit for brains detective investigating his death, alright? This is what happens when you're the best, Van Hatcher. The case is yours."

65

"What can you tell us about him?" asked Vanessa.

"Tom? Like I said, he was my best friend. We were assigned to the same residential house at Harvard and were on the same floor freshman year. His current business partner lived there as well: Charles Cole. I knew him too.

"Tom and I bonded over sports. I played football and he played tennis. There are a lot of demands on an athlete's time that regular students don't have. That's amplified even more at a place like Harvard where there are no easy classes or breaks for kids playing sports.

"But anyway," the commissioner continued, "I saw him on the dorm hall and then in the gym, said hi, and that was it. Friends ever since. He was the one who convinced me to move back to New York after graduation." Clark smiled. "Even though he thought I was crazy for joining the department. He wanted me to go to business school with him so we could open up shop together."

"Why did you go to the Academy, sir?" asked Dennis.

"My grandfather was a police officer on Long Island. Deputy Chief," Derrick said with pride. "He was the big male role model for me growing up, and I always wanted to be like him. People told me I was crazy. Tom included. Said I'd be wasting my degree." He paused. "I never felt that way. I was the first in my family to go to college, let alone go to Harvard. I'd already done them proud simply by graduating." Clark shrugged his shoulders. "Besides, I guess you can take the boy out of the working class but you can't take the working class out of the boy.

"Tom and I stayed friends, though. I was best man at his wedding. He was mine. Our kids grew up together. Our wives are friends." He shook his head and looked down at his desk. "I've been on that boat. In those islands. They said that the last time anyone saw him, he was up on the top deck looking out at the water. I've been there. In that exact spot. With him." Derrick sighed. "It makes no sense. He was so young. So loved, beloved, *revered* really. That's your job,

Van Hatcher. Find me an answer. Make it all make sense."

TWENTY-ONE

"How long have you known Commissioner Clark?" Vanessa asked as she and Dennis made the short walk from 1PP back to the 5th Precinct.

"He was my first captain," Dennis replied. "So twenty-two years."

"Have you ever seen him like that?"

"Never. I knew he and Tom Wilson were close, but no. He's really hurting."

"Which puts even more pressure on us to crack the case," Vanessa said.

"Clark wants answers. I can't blame him. If I had a brother, or a best friend who was like a brother, I'd want answers too."

The detectives arrived at their office in Chinatown ten minutes after leaving 1PP. The 5th Precinct was a cream-colored stucco-esque structure with four stories above ground (five stories total) and an old-fashioned, wrought iron fire escape down the center of the building. Window air conditioning units scattered throughout the office, and visitors were welcomed by pale blue double doors with '5th PRECINCT' written above them in large gold font.

The Lower East Side neighborhood had undergone massive gentrification in the past several decades, but it retained a 'come as you are' attitude that appealed to Detective Van Hatcher. Although it wasn't the most active area for crime, Commissioner Clark had assigned Dennis to the 5th so he would be close to 1PP.

"Why didn't he just put you at headquarters?" Vanessa asked. "Make you into a roaming, big cases only type detective?"

Dennis shrugged. "Beats me. But I like the 5th. We get a solid variety of cases, and I know Clark will hand me a few high-profile investigations too."

"What about you?" he asked when they reached their desks on the fourth floor. "Ever wish you were assigned somewhere flashier?"

"You may not know this, but for a junior detective I already have the most coveted spot in the department."

"The 5th is the most coveted spot?"

"No. Being your partner is."

Dennis turned to the side so she couldn't see him blush at the compliment. "Yeah, well, let's see if you can live up to the hype on this case."

"I know Wilson was the commissioner's friend and everything," Detective Smith said, "but aside from that why is he so important? People die all the time."

"You've been at this too long, V. You're getting too cynical."

Vanessa rolled her eyes. "You're one to talk. But seriously – what's the big deal about Thomas Wilson II?"

"Not one big deal; 200 million big deals."

"He's worth $200 million?"

"Yep. With the other boat passengers – his wife and kids – standing to inherit it all. A person can find a whole lot of motive in $200 million."

****

Despite the media coverage and the pressure from 1PP, Dennis and Vanessa attacked the Wilson investigation like they would any other suspicious death.

The detectives' attention focused on the people who had the best opportunity to kill Tom: his family and the yacht crew. His two granddaughters, Madison and Harper, were excluded due to their ages, but bank accounts, phone records, credit reports, and a host of other information was gathered on all nine initial suspects: MaryJo, Tripp, Anya, Kay, Luke, Ryan, Ship, Marcelo, and the cook, Serena.

"We'll need to interview all of them," Dennis said while

reading MaryJo's credit report. "Damn, these people spend a lot of money."

"I'll trade financials for phone records," Vanessa replied. "It's going to take me a week to get through all of the teenage son's text messages. And half of them are just little black boxes because the emoji didn't transfer over into the report."

"No dice," Dennis said with a smile. "Phone records are yours." The veteran detective took off his suit jacket and rolled up his sleeves.

Across the aisle at her desk, Vanessa had to admit that her partner could have a rugged, street-wise appeal to him when he wanted to. *No wonder the rookies all fall for him,* she thought. *Good looking and a rock star in the police department. Hell, if I had been single, I probably would've dated him too.*

"Hmm, that's interesting," Dennis said.

"What?"

"This charge on the son's credit card bill."

"Which son?"

"The older one. Tripp. He was charged $600 by a Dr. Ben Johnson in Westchester. A fertility doctor."

Vanessa shrugged her shoulders. "Looks like it worked since his wife is pregnant."

"Yeah, but . . ."

"But what?"

"That's like one doctor's visit, right? Where are the rest? My ex-wife and her husband did IVF, and she said it cost upwards of $30,000. Not a one-off charge of $600."

Vanessa leaned back from her desk and stared at her partner. "*You* were married?"

"A long time ago. That's beside the point. Make a note to ask Tripp Wilson about the clinic, ok?"

"Done."

A few minutes later, Dennis walked over to Vanessa's desk and placed a file in front of her. "Check it out."

70

Vanessa scanned the documents. "This is all current?"

"Yep. Remember how I said you can find a lot of motive in $200 million?"

She nodded. "No kidding. Especially since this shows that his daughter and son-in-law are drowning in debt."

"Looks like we may have ourselves a lead suspect."

****

Day turned to night while the detectives continued to scour through mountains of information in both paper and electronic form.

"Have you finished looking through those phone records?" asked Dennis. He glanced up at the clock on the wall. *1:30am.*

"Yeah." Vanessa nodded and yawned. "Nothing. I also looked through the vic's phone. The police in the Bahamas were smart and got his wife to tell them the password to unlock it. Lots of calls and texts to Mrs. Wilson and people at his office. His kids. Commissioner Clark. A few clients and charities. Seriously . . . nothing that jumps out at me."

"The world's most boring millionaire," Dennis said. "It looks like the only spontaneous thing this guy ever did was die."

TWENTY-TWO

"Tell me something good . . ." Dennis sang as he walked into the medical examiner's office several hours later. It felt like the next day to him, even though he didn't leave the precinct until 2:30 that morning. "Tell me that you found the killer yeaaahhh."

Sarah Templeton, the medical examiner, looked up from her computer screen and raised questioning eyebrows toward Vanessa.

"Nothing can explain him," Detective Smith replied. "I stopped trying a long time ago."

"Oh come on, ladies." Walking over to stand at the foot of the exam table holding Mr. Wilson's body, Dennis added: "it's a great day to be alive. Wouldn't you agree, Thomas?"

"I'm sure he would," Dr. Templeton said, "but I'm not so sure Officer Kozack will agree after your date tonight."

Van Hatcher turned to the medical examiner in surprise. "How did you –"

"Water cooler gossip. And your off-key singing confirmed it."

"So you finally convinced her to go out with you, huh?" Vanessa asked.

"Yup. Tonight." Dennis flashed a grin. "Gonna be great."

Vanessa rolled her eyes. "What do you have for us, Sarah?" she asked, hoping to change the subject.

"Getting Mr. Wilson's medical records was a bit of a hassle. His attorney is the executor of his estate and the only one legally authorized to act on behalf of the deceased's privacy rights. Apparently Mr. Wilson mandated that they wait ninety days after his death before reading his will, and the attorney kept arguing that the medical records should fall under that ninety day hold as well."

"That's stupid."

"I eventually talked him into agreeing to the release. And, of course, it was a dead end. No pun intended. Wilson was incredibly healthy – healthier than a lot of people ten or fifteen years younger than him. No major surgeries, no medications except a sleep aid . . . the guy was the picture of health."

"What about the autopsy?" asked Vanessa.

"It wasn't conclusive. There were signs of cardiac arrest as well as clear evidence of drowning. Sea water in the lungs and chest cavity. There's no way to know which came first, though, or if they happened simultaneously. I put a rush on the toxicology screen but it'll still take some time to get that back.

"He had fresh stitches on his left hand," the M.E. continued, "but all of the witness reports indicate that he cut his hand on a broken glass and was stitched up by a nurse on one of the islands. There were no signs of struggle . . . no other cuts or bruises around his wrists or neck, for instance. The only real abnormality was some bruising around his groin.

"If you look here," the doctor said, lifting up the sheet covering Wilson's body, "there's a large, rectangular bruise running along the upper inside of his left thigh."

"Could kicking or punching cause a bruise like that?"

"Probably not. As you can see, this mark is longer and narrower than a shoe or fist would leave behind."

"Vic gets in an argument with somebody on the boat," Dennis suggested, "that person decides to get even, wacks him in the groin with a metal pipe, and pushes him overboard."

Dr. Templeton shrugged her shoulders. "It's possible. But pretty much anything is possible at this point. I know he wasn't shot. I know he wasn't stabbed. Beyond that – it's really too early for me to say."

"Alright. Keep us updated. Let us know when the tox screen comes back."

"I will," the M.E. replied. "Oh, one more thing. Can you get me the contact information for the deceased's immediate family members?"

"Why?"

"I'd like to run some genetic testing to rule out rare diseases and things of that sort."

Dennis nodded. "Sure. I'll put you in touch."

TWENTY-THREE

The detectives had their first status meeting with Commissioner Clark that afternoon.

"Is he usually this hands-on with cases?" Vanessa asked while they waited in the hallway outside Clark's office. Even though she and Dennis had been partners for several years, this was the first time she was brought in on a special project for the commissioner.

"Never," Dennis replied. "Just be glad he wasn't a detective earlier in his career. Then he'd really be all up in our business."

"What business?" Derrick asked as he opened the door.

"Nothing sir," Van Hatcher replied with a smile.

"Come on in. Bring me up to speed."

"We've reviewed the phone records and financials for everyone who was on the yacht. All of the family members and the crew. We have a few questions and a couple potential leads, particularly with regard to the daughter's finances. But nothing stands out as a smoking gun."

"My assistant said you got the autopsy results back."

"Yes sir. Unfortunately, they were inconclusive. There's evidence of drowning and a heart attack and some bruising on one of his legs, but no obvious cause of death."

"Mystery on the high seas," the commissioner replied. "It's like Natalie Wood all over again."

"Who?" asked Dennis.

"I knew Detective Smith wouldn't get the reference but I figured you would, Van Hatcher. You're not *that* young . . . even if the rookies you date are."

Dennis' face turned beet red and his jaw dropped. "I . . . I . . ."

"No need for explanations," replied Commissioner Clark, waving it off with his hand. "You're all adults. As long as it doesn't interfere with your work." He paused and took a sip of coffee. "Natalie Wood," he continued, "was an actress. A very famous actress. Nominated for several Academy Awards."

"She was the little girl in the original 'Miracle on 34th Street'," Vanessa said.

Dennis turned and looked at his partner in surprise.

"What?" she asked. "I like old movies."

"That's right. I had forgotten about her early roles," the commissioner replied. "Anyway, several decades ago – late seventies, early eighties . . . sometime around then – Natalie Wood, her husband, and a couple other people sailed out on a yacht off Catalina Island. She went missing overnight, and they found her body the next morning."

"Everyone else on the boat denied any involvement," Vanessa said, "but her husband was – and is – the main suspect. He later admitted that they had a fight before she went missing."

Commissioner Clark nodded in agreement. "The official cause of death was drowning and hypothermia, I think."

"Didn't they reopen the case not too long ago?" Vanessa pulled her cell phone out of her pocket and started typing. A few seconds later, she said: "yep, here it is. The case was reopened in 2011 after the ship's captain admitted that he originally lied to the police. He said Natalie and her husband had a big fight and that he thought the husband killed her. The official cause of death was changed to drowning and other undetermined factors, and the husband continues to deny any wrongdoing."

"So they think the husband did it but can't prove anything," Dennis concluded. "If we're looking for parallels, that would make Mrs. Wilson the prime suspect. We don't know what's in his will, but logic says she'd inherit most of the estate."

"Regardless of who your suspects are," said Derrick, "I don't want this case ending up like the Wood one. I want every factor determined, you hear me?"

"Yes sir," the detectives replied in unison.

"Good. To that end, I'm sending you to the Bahamas to investigate."

"What?"

"The Wilsons were already cleared by the Bahamian police so they arrived back in the city this morning," Clark said, "but there's plenty of time for you to talk to them once you get back. I want you interviewing the crew, the detectives down there, any witnesses, the coroner . . . everybody."

"When do we leave?"

"Now. You're booked on the six o'clock out of LaGuardia. Better hurry so you won't be late."

****

After jogging from 1PP back to their office, Dennis headed straight for his department-issued car parked on the street outside the precinct. "I've gotta go home to get some clothes. You should too. We'll meet at the airport."

Van Hatcher jumped in his 2008 Ford Taurus and drove in the direction of the Manhattan Bridge. Twenty minutes later, he double parked in front of his building in Brooklyn and took the stairs two-by-two. Instead of going to his apartment, though, Dennis stopped at the unit belonging to his landlady.

"Mrs. Cheng. Hi. I have a huge favor to ask. Can you follow me up to my apartment so I can explain? I'm sorry but I'm in a hurry."

While Dennis struggled to pack a travel bag, not knowing how long his trip to the islands would last, he laid out his request.

"Would you mind –"

"Watching your cat while you're gone?" the older woman said, finishing his sentence.

"Could you? That would be fantastic. My boss sprung

this trip on me at the last minute. I'll leave enough food and water in the kitchen for three days, but I'm hoping to be home in two," Dennis said, trekking back and forth across his bedroom as he threw clothes in a duffle bag. "And the litter box is clean. But if you could just –"

Mary Cheng reached out and grabbed her favorite tenant's arm as he scurried by. "I'll check on him twice each day. Don't worry," she said, smiling toward the cat who had jumped onto the bed and was lying on top of Dennis' travel clothes. "Murphy and I are old pros at this."

Dennis stopped packing, looked at Mrs. Cheng, and sighed. "I know. That's the part that kills me. I hate having to leave him for such long periods."

Mary smiled and shook her head. "If the officers at your precinct could see you like this, fussing over a cat . . ."

Van Hatcher's face turned pale. "Which is why they never will." Walking over to the bed, Dennis reached down and lifted the black and brown ball of fur off his duffle bag, raising him up to cuddle under his chin.

"You be a good boy," the hard-nosed detective cooed. "I'll be back soon. Two, three days tops." Looking over at his landlady, Dennis said: "I'll call if we're going to be any longer than that. There's plenty of food and fresh litter in the pantry if he needs it."

Mrs. Cheng nodded her head. "We'll be fine. Now come here, Mr. Murph," she said, taking the cat into her arms. "Let your daddy go to work."

Dennis slung his duffle bag over his shoulder, gave Murphy one last pat on the head, and strode down the hall and out the front door.

"He's a funny one," Mrs. Cheng said to the cat who had jumped down and was figure-eight weaving his way through her legs. "No long term relationships. Shows no interest in having kids of his own."

"Meow," Murphy protested from the floor.

"Human kids of his own," the landlady corrected herself.

"But here he is gushing over leaving you for forty-eight hours." Mary shook her head. "Men. Go figure."

****

Half an hour away in the South Bronx, Vanessa walked through the front door of her apartment and was surprised to see her husband sitting on the couch.

"Why are you home?" she called out as she headed for the bedroom.

Roman Smith looked at his wife, confused. "Where else would I be?"

"Work," Vanessa replied, as puzzled by her husband's tone as he was by her question.

"It's summer. No school."

Vanessa stopped digging through her closet and leaned back on her heels. "Oh, right," she said, glancing over her shoulder to see her husband standing in the doorway. "Sorry. Didn't think about that."

"You never do."

"I don't have time for this right now," she said, continuing to put shoes, shirts, pants, and other necessary items into her suitcase. "The commissioner booked us on a six o'clock flight. I've gotta get packed and get to the airport."

"It's always something," Roman replied, frustrated to the point of picking a fight even when he knew he wouldn't win. "A meeting here, an interview there. And if the commissioner said it . . . woah," he added, throwing his hands up in mock surrender.

"It's not like I get to pick and choose when people get murdered, okay? This is what I do. You knew that when you married me. *Before* you married me. This is my job."

"But it shouldn't be your life," Roman said. He walked over and zipped up the suitcase, lifting it off the floor.

Mr. and Mrs. Smith marched side by side in silence out

of their apartment, down the hall, and onto the elevator – the sound of the wheels squeaking into the otherwise empty air.

Vanessa unlocked her car and Roman placed her suitcase in the trunk. "I love you, baby," he said, "but it's your job. It shouldn't be your life."

TWENTY-FOUR

"What's your problem?" Vanessa asked, sitting down next to her partner on the airplane.

"I called Carrie Kozack on my way over here," Dennis replied with a frown. "I worked a solid three months to get her to go out with me. She finally said yes, and now I had to cancel."

"Don't worry," Vanessa said, patting him on the shoulder. "A new crop of rookies arrives every year."

"Yeah, but Kozack is hot. With a capital H."

Vanessa laughed. "You're a piece of work. I can't believe a woman once agreed to marry you."

Dennis nodded. "Ten years. The first few weren't so bad, either."

"What's she like?" asked Detective Smith, curious to learn what kind of person would willingly put up with her grouchy partner.

"Very nice. Smart. She was a buyer for some fashion something or other. Couldn't stand the stress of being a cop's wife. Not that I blame her," Dennis added. "She remarried about a year after the divorce. He works in pharmaceutical sales."

"You keep in touch?"

"Yep. I see 'em all once or twice a year. They have twin girls who are about eight or nine now. They call me Uncle Dennis. I'm better at that – the uncle role. I was never cut out for the husband or father thing."

Vanessa turned and stared.

"What?"

"I've never heard you talk about yourself like that. In the four years we've been partners, that's the most self-reflection and personal commentary you've ever given."

Dennis shrugged his shoulders and leaned further back in his airplane seat. "I don't like bringing personal stuff to work. Clouds my mind and I can't think like I need to."

This from the guy who has slept with half the female cops under age thirty, she thought. "Well, regardless, maybe you should try it a little more often. Might help improve your reputation around the precinct. You know . . . make you seem a little more human?"

Dennis shook his head. "I like my reputation just fine, thank you. I don't want to seem human. I want to be a machine. A perp-catching, crime-solving, rooking-bagging machine."

"Don't forget donut-eating."

"Hey, I've cut way back. But you're right, I do love donuts."

"If your ex was so normal," Vanessa said, returning to the previous topic, "why do you now only date women half your age?"

He shrugged. "No harm, no foul. Just a little bit of fun."

"One of these days, that 'no harm no foul' kind of fun is going to come back and bite you in the ass. It already would've if you weren't such a damn Sherlock on murder cases."

Dennis flashed his partner the same smile he usually reserved for his rookie targets. "I don't mind a little biting every now and then."

"Oh, gross. I don't want to hear that!"

Van Hatcher laughed. "You said it first."

Vanessa rolled her eyes. *How in the hell he ever made it through sensitivity training is beyond me. Then again, if he cracks this case it'll all be worth it . . . and he knows it.*

"Ever think of dating someone more appropriate? Maybe getting married again?" she pressed.

"No way. Like I said, it's not for me. Besides, marriage is no guarantee of happiness."

Vanessa's thoughts flashed back to her fight with her husband. "That's true," she said. "Were your parents married?"

"Forty-eight years before Dad passed. Mom worked as a secretary on and off. Dad was with the Port Authority." He shrugged. "I don't know. They lived, they died. The idea of being happy in the middle didn't ever seem to occur to them."

"That's sad."

"Maybe. Maybe not. You can't miss something you don't know you're supposed to have."

Dennis put his headphones over his ears, a signal to Vanessa that he was finished talking.

What a strange man, she thought. *Although I guess it kind of explains his behavior. If his parents weren't happy together, he never had anyone to look up to for a model marriage.*

Glancing to the side, Vanessa watched as her partner and mentor closed his eyes and bobbed his head to the music. *Whatever the reason, he's still a hell of a detective.*

TWENTY-FIVE

Detectives Smith and Van Hatcher arrived at Nassau's police headquarters shortly after eleven o'clock that night.

Two hours late, Dennis thought with a grumble as their taxi squeaked to a stop. Even with letters from Commissioner Clark and the head of the Royal Bahamas Police Force, the two NYPD detectives were still detained and questioned at the airport. Only a personal phone call from the local commissioner himself was able to get Dennis, Vanessa, and their service weapons past Royal Bahamian Customs.

'Royal Pain in the Ass' is more like it, Van Hatcher thought, stepping out into the humid night air.

"Does it ever cool off here?" Dennis asked the taxi driver.

"Dis is cool, man," he answered with a chuckle.

"Detective Van Hatcher! Detective Smith! Welcome!"

A portly man in his mid-fifties bounded down the short steps in front of the Central Division headquarters, a two-story, seafoam green building located in downtown Nassau.

"I once had to wear a bridesmaid's dress that was that color," Vanessa whispered to her partner. "Horrid. I hope they got a good deal on paint."

"I'm Superintendent Armstrong," the man added, extending a hand in greeting. "So sorry about the mix-up at the airport. Come on in. I just made some coffee. I know you'll want to work right away. Or if you –"

Dennis held up a hand in hopes his host might stop talking. Thankfully, he complied.

"Umm, Superintendent . . . ?"

"Armstrong."

"Right. Coffee sounds good, thanks. If you can also show us what you have so far?"

The Bahamian smiled and nodded his head. "I knew that's what you'd say. Americans always want to get to work

84

straightaway. And lots and lots of coffee. Always the same."

"You've worked with American police before?" Vanessa asked.

"Oh yeah. Lots. Never on a murder case, though. We're pretty excited about that."

Vanessa reached out and grabbed her partner by the arm, barely stopping Dennis from lifting the other man off the ground by his lapels to teach him a lesson about respecting the dead.

"Down boy," she whispered.

Superintendent Armstrong didn't notice, having walked ahead of his guests into the station's main room. Hardwood floors, white paint, and ceiling fans filled the large space. Desks arranged in an open floor plan were littered with paper and computers, and a smattering of officers toiled away on the night shift.

"This used to be a house," he said, looking around. "That explains some of the layout. If you'll follow me this way, I have us a briefing room reserved."

Walking beside her partner, Detective Smith could tell that he was still fuming about the superintendent's 'excited' remark. "I'm sure he didn't mean it like that."

"He sure as hell did," Dennis snapped. "He was smiling while he said it."

"Everything alright?" Armstrong asked, shutting the briefing room door behind them.

"Actually –"

"Yes," Vanessa said. "Everything's fine." *Making the guy angry or embarrassed won't solve anything*, she thought. *He probably already resents us coming in here on his turf.*

"Good. Coffee is over there in the corner. You each have a copy of the important records we've gathered so far. And our timeline of events is up here," he said, gesturing toward a chalkboard with names and times scribbled on it.

"We'll need to see all of the records," Dennis replied.

"Yes, like I said –"

"No, you said we have a copy of the 'important' records. I want to see them all. The originals. Your view of what's important and my view of what's important are likely very different."

Vanessa sighed and walked over to the corner to pour herself a cup of coffee. *It's gonna be a long night.*

"Right, okay," their host replied. "I can get those for you. You'll of course want to speak to Inspector Rolle. He's in charge of the investigation and will be here tomorrow morning."

Oh shit, Vanessa thought. *Here we go.*

Dennis set his jaw and took a deep breath. He closed the binder that he had opened and raised his eyes to look at his Bahamian counterpart. Technically, the other man outranked him, but Van Hatcher wasn't in the mood for technicalities.

"My partner and I flew down here at the personal request of the commissioner of the New York City Police Department. The finest police department in the United States and one of the finest in the world. When we got here, we were subjected to two hours of suspicion, derision, and interrogation," Dennis continued, his voice calm but laced with anger. "And now, at 11:30 at night, after the taxi ride from Hell and no offer of dinner from anyone, we arrive at a puke green police station to discover that you're 'excited' someone died and that the one person," he said, his voice now at full volume, "the one person we actually need to talk to isn't even fucking here! What the hell kind of shit show operation is this?"

The superintendent stared back at his American visitor in shock. "Umm . . ."

"What my partner means," Vanessa jumped in, "is that we would very much like to speak with this Inspector Rolle. Tonight, if at all possible. Perhaps while he's making his way here, you could point us in the direction of a restaurant or supermarket where we might get something to eat."

Armstrong looked back and forth between Dennis and

Vanessa, still taken aback by the former's outburst.

"Sure," he said. "I'll call Mario, I mean Inspector Rolle, right now. And I'll have one of my officers drive you to get some food. I'm sorry, I should've realized you'd be hungry."

"Was that outburst really necessary?" Vanessa asked after the superintendent scurried out of the room.

"Sets the tone. Lets him know we mean business."

"It also lets him know you're an asshole."

Dennis shrugged his shoulders. "If that's what it takes to get some food and some answers around here, then so be it."

TWENTY-SIX

Inspector Rolle turned out to be the Bahamian version of Dennis: smart, brash, and used to getting his own way.

"You got mad at da wrong guy, stupid," Rolle said when he arrived at the station. "Armstrong is a pushover. Pick on somebody ya own size, yah?"

Vanessa bit her lip to keep from laughing. *Looks like he's met his match,* she thought with a grin.

Ignoring the other man's comments, Dennis launched into his investigation. "I'm going to need a list of everyone who has worked on the case. Everyone who was on the boat and/or saw Tom Wilson while he was in the Bahamas. Including the fisherman who found the body and the coroner who performed the initial autopsy."

"I already talked to da crew an' da family," Rolle replied. "Ya can see for yaself . . . report lists it as an accident."

"I know what your report says. We're making our own. Our medical examiner is doing her own autopsy, and the State of New York will issue its own death certificate."

"Jus' cause you're from America ya think you're better than all of us."

Dennis shook his head. "I don't think I'm better than you."

Oh boy, here it comes, Vanessa thought.

"I know I'm better than you."

****

Bright and early the next morning, Van Hatcher and Smith returned to the police station to find the captain of *The Arvid* waiting for them.

"Blankenship Jones," he said, extending a hand in greeting. "I heard through da grapevine that two New York detectives were in town. Thought I'd save ya da trouble and come in here myself."

"We appreciate that, Mr. Jones," said Vanessa.

"Please, call me Ship. Everybody else does."

"A yacht captain named Ship?"

"Yessir. My mom's maiden name."

"Alright," Dennis replied. "Whatever works. Why don't you come into the briefing room so we can talk?"

"Actually, sir, I thought ya might wanna do da talkin' on da boat. I can drive ya there."

"Is she docked at the police marina?" Vanessa asked.

The captain shook his head. "No ma'am. She won't fit. We've got 'er back over at Atlantis in a corner slip. Under constant guard."

"Who's with the boat now if you're here?"

"My first mate, Marcelo."

"Okay then," Dennis said. "Let's go see this crime scene."

****

While Vanessa dusted the entire 121-foot yacht for fingerprints, Dennis sat down at the dining room table to interview the captain.

"How long have you been working for the Wilsons?"

"Ah, ever since they bought da boat," Ship replied in his English-Creole accent. "So about fifteen years."

"Did you ever witness any fights or other trouble between family members?"

"Nah. Nothin' out of da ordinary for a big family on a boat together for a week and a half. Little squabbles here an' there but nothin' big."

"What about this trip in particular?" asked Dennis. "Was anyone acting strangely or did anything happen that caught your attention?"

The captain took a deep breath and thought about his

answer. "The son-in-law was more, I don' know what you'd call it, pissy than usual. An' Mr. Wilson was drinkin' more than usual." Ship paused. "He also started prayin'."

"What do you mean, praying?"

"I make my mornin' inspections about 5:30 every day," Jones explained. "For fourteen years, everybody'd still be asleep. This year, Mr. Wilson was awake. Up on da top deck an' prayin'."

"Did he say what he was praying about?"

"Nope. An' I didn't ask. None of my business."

Dennis nodded and wrote down notes on the pad of paper in front of him.

"What about security cameras on the boat?" Vanessa asked while fingerprinting around them. "We'd like to see any footage you have from the trip – especially the night he disappeared."

Ship shook his head. "No footage. Da cameras are never on while da family is aboard."

"Was that something new for this trip?"

"No. Mr. Wilson's been that way ever since he bought her. Said he doesn't wanna be watched."

"Didn't he worry about the downsides?" Dennis pressed. "If something happened and the cameras could've helped?"

"Like what? Fallin' overboard an' dyin'?"

Van Hatcher was surprised by the other man's sarcasm. "I was thinking more along the lines of pirates or something like that, but yeah, this is the perfect scenario when camera footage would be useful."

"I don' think da idea of danger from within ever crossed Mr. Wilson's mind, ta be honest. An' as far as pirates are concerned," Ship said, "follow me."

The captain led the two detectives up to the bridge. He unhooked a mass of keys from his belt loop and used one to unlock a full-length cabinet on the wall. Inside was an arsenal of AR-15s, handguns, body armor, flares, and ammunition.

90

"Holy shit."

"My crew an' I have all been through tactical arms trainin' an' hand-to-hand combat trainin'," Ship explained. "Mr. Wilson was a crack shot an' kept a second, smaller supply in his stateroom. *Da Arvid* would be a pirate's worst nightmare."

TWENTY-SEVEN

After concluding their interviews with Ship, the first mate, and the cook, Dennis and Vanessa hopped a ride on a police transport plane to the small island of Eleuthera.

Fifty miles east of Nassau, Eleuthera was a thin strip of land 110 miles long and only one mile wide. Once a hotbed of military and scientific research activity, Eleuthera was now home to a mere 8,000 residents.

The detectives flew into Rock Sound International Airport and were picked up by the local sheriff.

"In da sixties an' seventies there were U.S. naval an' auxiliary air force bases here," the sheriff explained while he drove. "Assignment of a lifetime that would've been! They did electronics testing an' missile tracking an' stuff like that," he added. "Yep, this was a place ta be back before independence. Princess Diana even came ta Eleuthera once. But now it's mostly tourism. Nature enthusiasts an' such."

"Where did you find the body?" Dennis asked, uninterested in the history lesson.

"Ah, washed up near Bannerman Town. About thirty kilometers south of here."

"Can you translate that distance to American?"

The sheriff threw his head back and laughed, a booming sound that filled the small sedan. "Translate ta American. I like that!" He laughed again. "I'm gonna use that one. We have thirty minutes or so. Bannerman Town is at da southernmost tip of da island."

The fisherman who found Tom Wilson's body didn't offer much new evidence except to confirm that yes, he saw the body wash ashore and no, there wasn't anyone else around when it happened. The local coroner was even less help.

"Only dead bodies we get 'round here are natural deaths," he said while taking a drag from a cigarette. "Don'

92

even have a morgue 'cept da one at da funeral home, but that one was full-up. Had ta use a meat freezer at da butcher's shop ta hold da body."

Vanessa nodded. "We heard. What was the victim wearing when you first saw him?"

"Khaki pants. Blue shirt. Both were kinda ratty, but da sea will do that to ya. No shoes. Real nice watch." The man reached into his pocket and pulled out a Rolex. "I made sure ta hang onto it so it wouldn't go missin'. Folks get sticky fingers 'round stuff like that."

"You didn't give it to Inspector Rolle when you talked to him?"

"Haven't talked ta nobody but you."

The New York detectives sighed and shook their heads in unison.

"Thank you for the watch. And for your time. Sheriff, can you drive us back to the airport? We're flying to Staniel Cay next."

TWENTY-EIGHT

After meeting with the boat captain and crew, lead investigator, coroner, Coast Guard station chief, owner of the Staniel Cay Yacht Club, and man who found Tom Wilson's body – all in the span of thirty-six hours – Dennis and Vanessa decided to regroup and assess what they knew over lunch at one of Nassau's most famous tourist spots: Señor Frog's.

"How do you think the New York taxpayers would feel if they knew about our wild goose chase in the Caribbean?" Vanessa asked, sipping a margarita.

"Since we're in the Bahamas, I think the proper term would be fishing expedition," her partner replied. "They'd probably be pissed. Especially if they knew how little we've learned."

"And definitely if they saw us eating here," Vanessa added, looking around at the bikini-clad tourists mingling under signs such as 'clothing optional beyond this point' and 'conserve water, drink tequila'.

Van Hatcher laughed. "You have a point there."

Both detectives stopped talking when their food arrived. The investigation schedule was so hectic that neither had eaten a full meal since their drive-thru tacos the night they arrived in Nassau.

"What a shitty situation," Vanessa said a few minutes later between bites of a hamburger.

"Aren't all of our murder cases shitty situations?"

"Yeah, they are. But this one especially. The more I find out about the guy," Vanessa said, "the more I like him. Obviously he was super smart and successful, but he was also big into charity work, loved his wife, and loved his kids. I mean, the number of lives he impacted – and for the better – is astounding."

"Doesn't hurt that he looked like a damn *GQ* model

either, did it?"

Vanessa smiled. "Well, no. That certainly doesn't hurt."

"I'll tell you one thing I like about this case," Dennis offered.

"What?"

"Everybody's cooperating. No chasing down witnesses who don't want to be found. No hours or days spent knocking on doors saying 'were you home, did you see anything'."

"That's true," Vanessa nodded. "Although sometimes those end up being the easier cases. We know the killer and it's just a matter of finding him. With this one, though, we've got all the pieces to the puzzle but are missing the most important part – the front of the box telling us what it's supposed to look like."

Vanessa took another sip of her margarita and leaned back in her chair. "I could get used to this, though," she said with a sigh.

"Oppressive heat, incompetent co-workers, and tourists drunk of their asses all the time?" Dennis shook his head. "No thanks."

"The heat does suck, but the police here aren't incompetent. They just work at a different pace than what we're used to. Plus, these drunks have nothing on the club scene in Manhattan on a Saturday night. Now come on," she added, "let's talk murder."

Dennis laughed. *I see the margarita is kicking in.*

"Well," he began, "if I had to summarize the trip, I'd say it was essentially pointless. Nothing I read in the files, saw on the boat, or heard from the witnesses suggests anything different than what we thought before we came down here."

"Cause of death: inconclusive," Vanessa said. "Why would Rolle list it as an accident, though?"

Van Hatcher reached out and pulled his partner's drink away from her. "Can she get a water, please?" he asked a passing waiter. "Thanks."

"What was that for?"

"You're asking stupid questions. Tequila brain won't help us. The police here called it an accident because they aren't looking for foul play – at least not like we are. They see a dead body and no signs of struggle, so they close the case and move on. No reason to linger. But the commish thinks his best friend was murdered, so we have to dig deeper."

"Yeah, I suppose . . ." Vanessa replied, still too drunk to be of any use to the conversation. She stared out at the clear blue water of the harbor and the long line of cruise ships docked in port. "I know why the Wilsons come here every year. It's gorgeous."

TWENTY-NINE

"Tell me you found our smoking gun."

Commissioner Clark looked across his desk the next morning at his lead detective, eager to hear Dennis' report from his trip to the Bahamas.

Detective Van Hatcher shook his head. "No sir. Unfortunately not. We were able to clear the crew of any suspected wrongdoing, though. They all sleep in one room on bunk beds, and the door squeaks like a motherf – it squeaks really, really loudly whenever it opens and closes," he said, catching his words in time. *No F-bombs in the commissioner's office*, Dennis reminded himself.

Derrick Clark's mouth twitched up in the corner. *Almost had ourselves a fun moment there.*

"Alright," the commissioner replied with a nod, "so it's not the crew. Which leaves the family."

"If anyone, yes sir."

"Get to it then," Clark ordered. "No stone unturned, Van Hatcher. No stone unturned."

****

On the fourth floor of the NYPD's 5th Precinct, Detective Smith was busy assembling the whiteboard for the Wilson case. A timeline of events, pictures of potential suspects, and any other pertinent information would be placed on the board so she and Dennis could see it all together at once.

With their background investigations complete, they were ready to begin questioning the main suspects: Tom Wilson's family.

Interviews always come after our research, Vanessa thought as she taped a picture of MaryJo to the whiteboard. *That way we don't tip off any of the suspects and can hopefully catch them off-guard with our questions.*

"Wadda we have?" Dennis asked, striding off the elevator toward his partner.

"First on my list is the wife," said Vanessa. "She likely stands to inherit the most from her husband's estate."

"Very true. Follow the money."

"Do you know how much we're talking about?"

Dennis shrugged his shoulders. "Not sure exactly. According to what the M.E. said, Tom Wilson's will won't be read until ninety days after his death." He paused. "He could've split it a lot of different ways, but $200 million is a lot no matter how you slice it."

Vanessa whistled. "Two hundred million dollars. That'd be nice."

"Not if it gets you killed."

She laughed. "You may have a point there." Vanessa pulled MaryJo's picture off the board to look at it more closely. "What I don't understand is why she would demand a separate investigation if it could call her inheritance into question? Insurance companies won't pay until any suspicious circumstances are resolved, and New York's slayer rule prevents people from inheriting the estate of the person they killed."

"If she did it, I doubt she expects to be caught. Plus, what a great way to throw us off the scent. How many times do we have a super cooperative spouse who ends up as the perp?"

Vanessa sighed. "A lot. But we have to investigate those cases. This one was a cut and dry natural causes/accident scenario. We're only looking into it because the dude was friends with the commissioner."

"You're right. I still say she's suspect number one, though. Follow the money . . . and she's gonna get a ton of it."

"What about the kids?"

"Commissioner Clark said that Wilson told him his wife

gets most of the money but his kids get a little bit. So the money incentive is still there, albeit less. The oldest son is actually at a disadvantage because of the death," Dennis concluded. "He worked for his dad's firm ever since he finished college. Now all of that job security is gone. The daughter and son-in-law are in deep with the credit card companies, so there's plenty of motive there. We need to learn more about the younger son, though."

Vanessa nodded in agreement. Stepping up to the whiteboard, under <u>Suspects</u> she wrote '1. wife; 2. daughter; 3. 2nd son'.

THIRTY

Uptown in Midtown, MaryJo Wilson was meeting with her husband's financial advisor and estate planner: Joe Tumlin. Kay joined her mom for emotional support.

"Mr. Wilson set you up well financially," the dually-licensed CPA and attorney said. "There won't be any problems with the bills or creditors during this ninety day hold period. After that, of course, you'll be free to go forward with things as you see fit."

"Why did Dad want us to wait?" Kay asked. "That doesn't make any sense."

"I generally counsel my clients to establish a waiting period of at least thirty days. The last thing we want is a grief-stricken spouse or child to blow through their inheritance because their family member died two days earlier and they don't know how else to deal with the pain."

MaryJo nodded. "Tom and I talked about that. I understand."

"What about the insurance money? Is that on hold too?"

"Yes," Tumlin replied, "but for a different reason. Since the cause of death is still inconclusive, at least from the NYPD's perspective, the insurance company is doing its own investigation to make sure the recipient isn't the murderer. Also to ensure that your father's death wasn't the result of his own criminal behavior. If it was, the claim will be denied."

"My dad was not a criminal!"

"Shhh, honey, it's alright. Nobody is saying he was." Turning to the lawyer, MaryJo said, "you told me on the phone that we needed to discuss the –" she paused as emotion caught in her throat – "the funeral arrangements?"

"Yes. We do. Tom left specific instructions for where and how he wanted to be buried." Tumlin passed an envelope to MaryJo. "It's all in there."

Mrs. Wilson opened the envelope and unfolded the letter

inside. Her eyes welled with tears as she scanned the page.

"This says . . . this says he wants his f-funeral to be at St. Monica's Church. I've never heard of it b-before."

"It's a Catholic church on East 79th. A beautiful building."

"But Dad's not Catholic."

"Your father was baptized Catholic as a baby," the lawyer explained. "I believe his maternal grandmother saw to it. He apparently came back around to the faith these past several months and was a frequent worshipper there."

"Why didn't he ever say anything about it to me?" asked MaryJo, reeling from the shock of her husband's secret life.

"I don't think Mr. Wilson was ready to tell you, ma'am. We all experience our faith in different ways."

****

Back home after her meeting with the lawyer, MaryJo began the difficult task of picking out Tom's suit for the funeral.

"We didn't talk about any of this," she said to an empty room. "What to wear. Where to have the service. Burial. Cremation. None of it."

MaryJo blinked to keep from crying. "We always assumed there was still time. He was so y-young." The newfound widow collapsed on her bed and curled into a ball. After a few minutes, the comforter was soaked through with tears.

"May I help, ma'am?" asked the housekeeper, Mrs. Mason.

MaryJo shook her head. "Not unless you can bring Thomas back to me."

Alice Mason sat down on the edge of the bed and gently stroked MaryJo's hair. "I'm so sorry, ma'am. I know how much you loved Mr. Wilson. And how much he loved you."

MaryJo sat up and nodded her head. "Thank you. You

meant a lot to him, too." She wiped tears from her cheeks and walked toward her husband's closet. "I need to pull it together. I still have to pick out his clothes for the funeral. Maybe this Desmond Merrion," she said, lifting a finely tailored Supreme Bespoke suit off the rack.

"He flew over to London for the fitting," MaryJo added, running her hands over the soft gray fabric. "This one. I think he'd like this one."

THIRTY-ONE

The toxicology report arrived at the medical examiner's office later that afternoon. The detectives joined the M.E. in her basement office to review it.

"What's it say?" asked Dennis.

"I kept wondering why sharks didn't get the body before it washed ashore," Dr. Templeton said. "But now I know that, unless the sharks were alcoholics, they wouldn't have wanted a piece of this guy. He had a .26 blood alcohol content."

"Holy shit."

"That would explain how he fell overboard," Vanessa said.

"The victim's tox screen also showed significantly elevated levels of Zolpidem in his system."

"What?"

"Zolpidem," the M.E. replied. "More commonly known as Ambien."

"Overdose?" Vanessa asked.

Templeton shrugged her shoulders. "It's possible. Ambien is a sleep aid, which means it's a hypnotic and alters people's thinking and reactions. Particularly in older patients, and even more particularly in patients who consumed alcohol at the same time that they took the drug. If someone combined the two at the levels our victim did, they would experience drowsiness, clumsiness, and poor motor control."

"So," Dennis proposed, "our guy gets trashed, pops a couple Ambien, stumbles around the ship, and falls overboard. Accident."

"He would have needed to do more than pop a couple of pills. Mr. Wilson was prescribed a ten milligram dosage, which is already the highest level recommended by the FDA. Most people take a 5mg pill, and some even split that 5mg pill in half. Based on the results of the tox screen, Wilson had five times the prescribed amount in his system."

"Fifty milligrams?" asked Vanessa, raising her eyebrows in surprise.

Templeton nodded her head. "Combine that with a Blood Alcohol Content of .26 . . ."

"How was this guy even functioning?" asked Dennis.

"We don't know that he was," Vanessa noted.

"Mr. Wilson was showing some early signs of liver damage. It's entirely possible that his alcohol tolerance was built up so high that .26 would barely faze him. But," the M.E. added, "when you combine that with the overdose on Zolpidem, you get a very dangerous situation."

"Deadly dangerous."

"Don't forget," the doctor said, "Wilson's heart also showed signs of cardiac arrest."

Dennis stopped scrolling through emails on his phone and looked up at the medical examiner. "Hold on. You're telling me that, based on the autopsy and the tox screen, this guy could've intentionally overdosed, accidentally overdosed, intentionally jumped overboard, accidentally fallen overboard, or had a plain ol' heart attack. Anything else you want to throw out there? Snake bite? Radiation exposure? Allergic reaction to shellfish?"

The medical examiner sighed. "I know the autopsy wasn't much help. I'm sorry. I can't tell you exactly why or how he died. But," she said, "I do know that he was alive when he hit the ocean. The seawater in his lungs proves that."

"Alright," Vanessa said, "give us your best guess. What do you think killed him?"

"Best guess? He got messed up on pills and booze, slipped on the deck, fell overboard, and the shock of hitting the water sent him into a panic. Then a combination of inhaled seawater and cardiac arrest killed him."

"No foul play?"

Dr. Templeton shook her head. "I don't see any signs of

it."

Vanessa nodded. "Okay. The vic was tennis partners with the commissioner so we've gotta look under every rock, you know?"

"Yep. I understand. But I really don't think there's anything here."

THIRTY-TWO

Detectives Van Hatcher and Smith rode the elevator from the basement up to their fourth floor office.

When they got to their desks, MaryJo was waiting on them.

"Mrs. Wilson," said Dennis, shaking her hand. "Thank you for coming in to speak with us."

MaryJo nodded but didn't respond.

"Right this way," Vanessa said, escorting their suspect to the interview room known as the witness box.

"From everything we've learned," Smith said, "your husband was like a god in this city. I can personally attest to the benefits of his generosity toward the Police Foundation. It must be such a terrible loss for you."

MaryJo again nodded her head in silence, staring at an unknown spot on the floor in front of her.

"We want to thank you for coming in today for the interview," Vanessa repeated. "It's standard procedure for us to talk to everyone who was there when it happened."

The widow bobbed her head up and down.

"I'm sorry, ma'am, but are you okay?" *She looks stoned,* Vanessa thought. When MaryJo didn't respond, the detective repeated: "ma'am? Mrs. Wilson?"

"What?"

"Are you alright?"

"I just finished picking out the last outfit my husband will ever wear. So no, I'm not alright. Can we just get this over with?"

"Sure," said Dennis, his curiosity piqued by the woman's strange behavior. "Why don't we start with what you remember from the night your husband died?"

MaryJo sighed and looked up at the ceiling. "Not much, really. We had dinner at Staniel Cay. Afterward, Thomas wrestled around on the floor with the girls for a little bit."

"'The girls' being your granddaughters?'"

"Yes. Madison and Harper. After that, things disbanded for the night. Kay and Luke went to bed, as did I. Anya had already gone to sleep earlier . . . the pregnancy has made her tired recently."

"What about your husband and sons?"

"They went to the top deck to drink whisky. It was Thomas and Tripp's ritual, and Ryan joined them that night."

"Their ritual this trip?" Vanessa asked. "Or every trip?"

"They've done it the past few years at least. I think it started after Tripp and Anya got married. Thomas always invited Luke, too, but he never joined them."

"Not a drinker?" asked Dennis.

"Luke drinks wine, not hard liquor. But he's always been kind of a loner. Not really a guy's guy in that way."

"Did Mr. Wilson and his son-in-law not get along?" asked Detective Smith.

"No, they got along," MaryJo said. "They weren't particularly close, but they got along."

"Were you and your husband aware of Mr. Eckersely's money problems?" Dennis asked.

MaryJo looked across the table. "What money problems?"

"A review of financial records showed that your son-in-law made some bad investments over the past few years. Luke also has quite a gambling habit. He and your daughter racked up a good bit of debt as a result."

MaryJo took a deep breath and tried to process the news. "I had no idea. Thomas never said anything about it, so I doubt he knew either." She shook her head. "They had to know we would've helped them. All they had to do – all they have to do now – is ask. Luke's a proud man, though," MaryJo added with a sigh. "Too proud for his own good."

Vanessa scribbled notes in her binder as fast as she could while Dennis considered which question to ask next.

The son-in-law angle is probably tapped out, at least for

now, he thought.

"You said that Mr. Wilson and your sons, Tripp and Ryan, went up to the top deck to have a drink after you went to sleep," Dennis began.

"That's right."

"What time was that?"

"Umm . . . we got back from Staniel about 9:30, so probably around 10 I would guess."

"And they would've been the last people to see your husband alive?"

"I suppose," said MaryJo. "I was out pretty much as soon as my head hit the pillow."

"Could Mr. Wilson have come into the room at some point and then left again without you noticing?"

MaryJo nodded. Her brown hair, dyed to cover the gray, swayed gently over her shoulders. "It's possible," she answered. "I felt a cold coming on so I took some Nyquil before I went to sleep. I usually enjoy the movement of the boat and the sounds from the water and engine at night, but I didn't want to be sick the rest of the trip."

"Is there anyone who can confirm that? Who saw you taking the medicine?"

"No. Although the bottle and the little measuring cup would've still been on the bathroom sink on *The Arvid*. I don't know if you took pictures of it or whatever."

Vanessa nodded. "We did. We'll check."

"Thomas hated all of the movement," MaryJo continued. "He took an Ambien every night on the boat to help him sleep. Said there was too much noise otherwise."

The detectives exchanged a quick glance.

"What? What was that look you two just did?"

"The toxicology report showed high levels of Ambien in Mr. Wilson's bloodstream," Vanessa replied.

"How high?"

"Higher than was prescribed, that's for sure."

MaryJo raised her hand up over her mouth. "What are

108

you saying? He overdosed?"

"We don't think so, no ma'am," said Dennis. "But mixing sleep aids with alcohol can be dangerous. Did anyone else know about your husband taking the Ambien?"

"I'm sure they did. It wasn't a secret."

"Okay," Dennis replied, jotting down notes. "We have to ask," he added, "how were things between you and your husband? Any trouble at home?"

"Things were fine. We'd been married thirty-seven years. We were a . . . we were a team."

"No problems?"

"None."

"Did Mr. Wilson have any enemies? Any business deals gone bad recently?"

"No. No . . . like you said, he was a god in this city." MaryJo sighed and smiled. "He wasn't always like that, you know. The refined, lord-of-the-manner business tycoon."

"He wasn't?"

"When we first met, Thomas was brash, opinionated, a perfectionist, and *obsessed* with making his own way. Outrageously competitive. Too competitive, really. He let his emotions get involved, especially if he lost."

"What happened? Why'd he change?"

"Time, mostly. Older and wiser." MaryJo smiled. "Becoming a dad made him take fewer risks and appreciate his own father more. He learned to channel his competitiveness into tennis and business." Her smile grew wider. "I always told him he was like George Clooney . . . better with age."

Dennis shook his head while Vanessa nodded hers in agreement with the analogy.

"Okay," Van Hatcher said, closing his notebook, "I know you're very busy with planning the funeral and all, so we'll let you go. It's possible we'll have some follow up questions for you later on."

"That's fine," Mrs. Wilson replied as she stood up from

her chair. "You know how to reach me. If there's anything you need, anything that would help . . . ." Her voice broke and tears caught in her throat. "L-let m-me know."

"We will. Thank you, Mrs. Wilson."

"I'll walk you out," Vanessa offered.

When Detective Smith returned from the elevators, she found her partner standing in front of the case's whiteboard.

"What do you think?"

"She doesn't strike me as a killer."

"Me neither."

Dennis erased MaryJo's name from the board, grabbed a marker, and wrote '1. daughter/son-in-law' at the top of the suspects list.

Vanessa nodded her head. "Agreed."

THIRTY-THREE

Two days later, Dennis walked into the precinct wearing a suit his partner had never seen before. Even though it was a Saturday, Vanessa and the rest of the detectives were all at work.

"Where are you going all dressed up?" she asked.

"Tom Wilson's funeral."

Smith laughed. "No, seriously."

"Seriously. It's very important to maintain a connection with the victim's family. They hear information from the street that would never reach us otherwise. Besides, what better way to feel out potential suspects? Fifty bucks says the killer attends the funeral."

"A, there's a 99% chance that Wilson's death was an accident." Vanessa grinned. "Get it – the 1% left over?"

Dennis rolled his eyes. "Yes. Funny."

"B, considering that the only people who could've killed him are the boat crew who we already cleared and his immediate family members, your bet isn't all that risky."

Van Hatcher smiled. "I don't make a bet if the odds are against me. There are still some non-family options, though. Delayed effects of poisoning. CIA hit."

"CIA?"

Dennis shrugged his shoulders. "Anything's possible at this point. But I gotta go. Time to see how the other half mourns."

****

Forty-eight hours after her interview with the police, MaryJo Wilson donned her best Chanel suit and rode sixteen blocks north to a church she'd never set eyes on before.

St. Monica's light brown, Gothic Revival façade opened to reveal a gorgeous interior sanctuary with wooden pews,

111

stained glass windows, and a beautiful marble alter at the front of the church. Small white flowers lined the ends of the pews, and one giant bouquet lay on top of the mahogany casket at the front end of the center aisle. Upon seeing her husband lying in repose, MaryJo broke down in tears.

"I still say we should've held the service at St. Patrick's," Kay whispered. "It can hold way more people."

Commissioner Clark and his wife had arrived early to support the family, and he shook his head in disagreement. "What we should be doing is what we are doing." Speaking to Kay like the surrogate daughter she was, he added: "this is what your father wanted."

"He's right," said Tripp. "How many people do we really need to make sure can attend? Fifty? A hundred? Certainly not the 2,000 or whatever it is that St. Patrick's will hold."

Derrick walked over and knelt in front of MaryJo, who had stayed silent during the entire conversation. Grasping her hands, the police commissioner said: "Tom developed a relationship with the people at St. Monica's. For whatever reason, he felt comfortable and welcome here. This is right – we're honoring his wishes."

MaryJo wiped tears off her cheeks. "We're burying my husband today. There's nothing right about that. But this is what Thomas wanted, so this is what he gets."

THIRTY-FOUR

As the mourners began to pour into St. Monica's, a crowd gathered outside the church to witness the spectacle. Some were curious passersby, but many were paparazzi, reporters, and other onlookers hoping to catch a glimpse of the celebrities in attendance.

The mayor of New York City, the governor of New York, three sitting U.S. senators, a former Miss America, and a Saudi prince were all among the guests offering their final respects to Tom Wilson.

Anthony Quinn, the reporter from Channel 3 who had been covering the Wilson story from the beginning, was also there broadcasting live.

"Security is extremely tight around St. Monica's Church today for the funeral of business tycoon and noted philanthropist Thomas Wilson II," Quinn said. "You'll recall from earlier broadcasts that the sixty-four year old Wilson, a New York native, fell overboard and reportedly drowned while vacationing on his family's yacht in the Caribbean. Dignitaries and celebutantes from across the country and around the world are expected to be in Manhattan today to offer their respects to the Wilson family, in addition to a veritable who's who of millionaires and billionaires from New York and beyond."

****

Inside the gothic cathedral, the guests milled around talking. If not for the casket in front of the alter, one could have been forgiven for mistaking the gathering for a social mixer. Most of the gossip centered on condolences for MaryJo and her kids, but some of the guests weren't as nice.

"A church funeral?" said LeeAnne Keys, a woman who sat on the board of the Metropolitan Museum of Art with the deceased. "Really? When's the last time Tom Wilson darkened the doorway of a church?"

"Oh come on," her friend and neighbor replied. "Give the guy a break. He is dead, after all."

LeeAnne lowered her voice and nodded her head toward the front of the sanctuary. "Did you see that the Police Commissioner is here?"

"No. Is he really?"

"Apparently, MaryJo isn't buying the drowning story. Tom was friends with the commissioner, so she's making him investigate it like a murder."

"Seriously?"

LeeAnne nodded. "We all saw the story about how much they donated to the Police Foundation last year. I don't think Clark has a choice."

"Probably. Plus, it is weird for Tom to die so suddenly like that. He was in fantastic shape."

LeeAnne made an appreciative murmur. "He sure was. The city got uglier on average without him here to set the curve."

****

At the other end of the center aisle, MaryJo watched the gossiping women out of the corner of her eye, judging them as harshly as they were judging her.

LeeAnne Keys knows better than to show up in that color, she thought, her eyes scanning the hunter green wrap dress that the other woman was wearing. *I don't care what fashion magazines say. You wear black to a funeral.*

MaryJo was charitable toward the less fortunate but tolerated no dissention within the ranks of the upper class. Trained early in the art of Southern insults, wherein the speaker makes the recipient feel like they're receiving a compliment instead of a verbal slap, Mrs. Wilson pulled no punches when faced with a peer who wasn't living up to

114

standards.

"I understand if you can't afford it or you never had anyone teach you the proper way," she whispered to her daughter, Kay. "That's not your fault . . . this is a different world and we have customs and expectations that outsiders can't understand. But someone like LeeAnne Keys? She went to Radcliffe, for crying out loud. She's on the board at The Met, her mother chaired the Foundation for the Arts, and her father was a surgeon at Mount Sinai. She should know better."

THIRTY-FIVE

Standing beside the closed casket, MaryJo looked like Jackie Kennedy reincarnated. From her knee-length black shift dress to her black gloves and lace veil, Mrs. Wilson was the picture of mourning couture. The only color in her clothes, people noticed, was the occasional flash of red from the soles of her Christian Louboutin pumps.

"I bet her outfit alone cost $3,000," whispered Alexa, an associate at Wilson|Cole. "Don't even get me started on what they must've forked over for all the flowers and the security detail out front."

"I think the flowers look nice," her co-worker, Kourtney, replied, looking around the sanctuary full of elegant white roses, orchids, and tulips that stopped tastefully short of bridal. "Mrs. Wilson looks beautiful, as always."

Alexa rolled her eyes. "You don't have to suck up now. Tom can't hear you."

"Don't be so callous. This is a funeral. A funeral for the man who gave both of us a shot in investment banking . . . and paid the salary that bought those Jimmy Choo's on your feet."

Her co-worker opened her mouth to respond but was interrupted by their arrival at the front of the receiving line. Stepping forward, first Alexa then Kourtney shook hands with the widow and offered their condolences.

"I'm very sorry for your loss," Alexa said. "Mr. Wilson was a great boss. We're all going to miss him terribly at the office."

MaryJo nodded her head in thanks.

"I can't even imagine what this must be like for all of you," Kourtney added. "Such a senseless tragedy." Unlike her colleague, Kourtney was sincere. She worshipped Tom and still harbored a not-so-secret crush on the handsome businessman.

116

"It is," MaryJo replied in reference to her husband's tragic death. "Thank you both for being here. I know Thomas would've appreciated it."

"Of course," Alexa said with a sympathetic smile.

Stepping forward, she placed her hands on Tripp Wilson's arms and kissed him on the cheek. Alexa and Tripp had enjoyed an on-again off-again romance before he met Anya, and the two co-workers remained close friends.

"I'm so sorry," she said. "We all loved your dad."

Tripp sighed and bit his lip to help hold back tears. "Thanks. Thanks for coming. You too, Kourt. It means a lot."

"He meant a lot of all of us," Kourtney replied, ignoring the smirk on her friend's face. *Even if I didn't have a crush on him, he still would've meant a lot to me*, she thought.

"If there's anything you need at the office or anything we can do to help, call me. Okay?" said Alexa, reaching out to hold hands with Tripp.

"I will."

Ten feet away, seated on the first pew, Anya frowned while watching the exchange between her husband and Alexa. Sensing someone beside her, the younger Mrs. Wilson turned to see Cindy Clark, the police commissioner's wife, sitting down next to her.

"How are you holding up, dear?"

"I'm fine," Anya replied. "The baby makes me tired, so I can't stand up there the whole time."

Cindy nodded her head in understanding. "I was exhausted the first two trimesters. Both times. It got better in the third trimester, though." She paused. "He was never in love with her, you know."

"What?"

"Tripp and Alexa," Cindy said, motioning her head toward where the two were standing. "He was never in love with her. Not like he loves you."

"I know," said Anya, placing a protective hand over the small bump on her stomach. "I just wish he wasn't so

117

friendly with her."

"Did you tell him that?"

"No." Anya shook her head. "He'll say I'm being paranoid and hormonal."

"Probably," Cindy replied, then smiled. "I've been married for thirty-four years, I've raised a son, and my husband works in a profession that's 87% male. Trust me on this. Tripp may call you paranoid and say you're hormonal, but the next time little-miss-thing over there goes to kiss him on the cheek and hold his hands, he won't let her. Men are great at fixing problems, but you have to make them aware of it first."

Cindy patted the younger woman on the knee. "Trust me," she repeated. "Speaking of men, Derrick is waving me over. I'll see you again later, honey."

****

Near the casket, standing guard with his mom and siblings, Tripp spotted Detective Van Hatcher lurking at the rear of the church.

"What is he doing here?" he muttered under his breath.

"Who?" Kay asked, following her brother's gaze.

"See the guy in the back with his tie askew, hands in his pockets, trying to blend in?"

"The one in the cheap suit with the $5 haircut and $10 shoes?"

Tripp nodded. "That's the one. He's the detective assigned to Dad's case. I thought Derrick told him to stay away from the funeral," he added as he walked toward the interloper.

"Hold on," Kay said, walking as fast as her four-inch heels could carry her. Mrs. Eckersely caught up to her brother right after he arrived in front of the detective.

Van Hatcher extended his hand in greeting, and Tripp reluctantly shook it. "What are you doing here?"

"I came to pay my respects to your father."

"You didn't know him."

"If you want to respect him," Kay said, "you should find out who killed him."

"I don't believe we've met," Dennis replied, unfazed by the Wilsons' rude behavior. "I'm Detective Van Hatcher. Commissioner Clark assigned my partner and me to investigate your father's death."

Kay folded her arms across her chest and lifted her chin. "He also told you not to come today."

"Look, everyone who knew, worked with, loved, or hated your father is here right now in this church. You can't honestly expect me to stay away." He paused. "I'm not intruding. I'm not bothering anybody. In fact, I didn't even speak to anyone until you two came over and started talking to me."

"What do you want?" asked Tripp.

The detective shrugged his shoulders. "Something to work with. Anything. Tell me about your dad," he prompted. "Was he the super involved, little league coach type? Distant workaholic? Somewhere in between?"

"Why do you need to know that?"

"It helps me to have a full picture of who the victim was. That way, I can find anything that doesn't seem to fit the narrative."

"He was somewhere in between," answered Kay, glancing over her shoulder at her father's casket. "Closer to the workaholic side, but he got better as we got older."

Tripp nodded in agreement. "He was really good with the big stuff. Either that or his assistant was good at reminding him about the big stuff."

"It was like he knew he couldn't miss those things without causing serious damage," his sister said.

"Every year on our birthdays," Tripp continued, "either the weekend before or the weekend after was 'Dad Time'. He'd pick something we loved to do and make a big event of it. My birthday is at the end of October and I love baseball, so we'd fly to wherever the World Series was and go to a game together."

Kay smiled and nodded her head. "I did dance for twelve years, so mine was always Opening Night of The Nutcracker. Dad would send a car to pick me up from Miss Porter's, which was great because it meant an extra trip home during the semester. Even though the show was in the city, we'd still make a night of it. Dinner beforehand; a stretch limo to drive us there." She sighed. "My fifteenth birthday was the best. I guess he figured that I would want a big party for my Sweet Sixteenth and would be too old for all of it on my seventeenth – both of which, of course, were true – so he made my fifteenth extra special.

"He flew us over to St. Petersburg, Russia and we saw The Nutcracker there. 'As Tchaikovsky meant for it to be seen'," she explained, imitating her father's deep voice. Tears filled Kay's eyes. "He did the big stuff well."

"And the not-so-big stuff?" asked Dennis.

"Dad missed a lot of that," Tripp admitted. "He probably missed more than he made, but he was there when it really counted. I'll give him that."

"He was a wonderful grandfather," Kay said. "He loved having grandkids. My girls adored him."

Tripp nodded in agreement. "I was looking forward to seeing him with mine and Anya's baby. To talking with him about dad stuff, you know? Father to father. Things he did, things he would've done differently, lessons learned." Tripp lowered his eyes to the floor. "That would've been nice to have together."

****

After Tripp and Kay walked away to rejoin their mom, Derrick Clark took his turn to have words with the funeral crasher.

"Commissioner, sir."

"Detective Van Hatcher," Clark said, shaking his hand. "I didn't expect to see you here."

Dennis shrugged his shoulders and looked around. "Thought it would give me a good lay of the land. People love to gossip at funerals. Say things they might not during a more formal interview."

"True. Alright. As long as you're only observing. I don't want anything upsetting MaryJo or the kids today."

"Understood, sir."

Hoping to find a seat near the back of the church, Van Hatcher was surprised to see Blankenship Jones in one of the pews.

"Captain. This is a surprise."

"Please, call me Ship," he said, sliding over so Dennis could sit next to him. "It was kinda a last minute, spur-of-da-moment thing. Mr. Wilson was a good boss, ya know? I feel terrible that all of this happened on my watch. Jus' terrible."

Dennis laughed. "Okay man, for real, where are you from?"

"Waddaya mean?"

"At first I thought I was getting a British vibe, but then it sounded more American. Plus there's an island flair going on . . . I've never met anybody else who talks like you do."

Ship smiled. "Thank ya, I think. You're correct on all fronts, actually. My parents were English an' I grew up there. But my whole adult life I've been in da Caribbean, captainin' a yacht owned by Americans. So ya . . . all of da above."

"Registration records showed that you're the previous owner of *The Arvid*. Why didn't you tell us that when we interviewed you?"

"Dunno. Didn't seem important."

"That's a mighty interesting motive, if you ask me. Rich guy pretends to be poor. Drives a boat for a while, then gets fed up with people ordering him around when he's worth three times what they are."

Jones shook his head. "No way. Like I said, Tom Wilson was a good boss. You're right – *Da Arvid* used ta be my boat. She originally belonged ta my grandparents.

"Our family home in England was Arvid Hall," he explained. "My dad didn't like da boat, got seasick or somethin', so my grandfather left it ta me in his will. I sailed her 'round for a couple years, but after my dad died I learned some things 'bout my family history that I'm not proud of. Ownin' sweatshops in Manchester an' investin' in slave plantations in da Indies before that." Ship shook his head. "A lot was s'posed ta fall on my plate as head of da family, but I decided ta chuck it all an' do what I loved. Arvid Hall is now a girls' school, da money is in a blind trust, an' as far as most people know, I'm a sea captain. Nothin' more, nothin' less."

THIRTY-SIX

Although both of Tom's parents were already dead, his sister and her husband flew in from California for the funeral. Claire Wilson Friedman was two years younger than her brother and an executive at Google. Although her inheritance and her husband's salary as a doctor meant she didn't need to work, Claire was a disciple of the 'lean in' philosophy. Shunning all of the pretense that surrounded elite East Coast society, she was only half-joking when she said that she went to Stanford as a way to escape New York.

Claire's only son (and Tom's only nephew), Rich, was a junior associate at a top law firm in Chicago. His boss initially refused to give him time off for the funeral, but he changed his mind after learning that the young man's uncle was *the* Tom Wilson.

"It makes me sick," Rich told his mom with disgust. "Expecting me to turn my uncle's funeral into a business mixer for potential clients."

"Don't be so offended. That's the only reason half of these people are here. To see and be seen."

"You're joking."

"Nope," Claire said, scanning the crowd to find her sister-in-law. "That, and to be able to mention it in conversations for the next six months. 'When I was at Tom Wilson's funeral blah blah blah'. Oh, there she is," she added, spotting MaryJo at the front of the church. "Come on."

A few minutes later, MaryJo's father and his second wife arrived at St. Monica's. Winfred Fisk lived six blocks away from his daughter but only saw her two or three times per year, usually at society events hosted by others. A large part of the gulf in the Fisk family had to do with the scantily-clad blonde clinging to the old man's arm.

"Such a cliché," MaryJo hissed, watching her elderly

father make his way to his seat with the step-mom who was younger than she was. "Half the time I think he married her so he could have a full-time physical therapist without having to pay her."

"Maybe he did," Kay replied. Her grandfather looked ridiculous parading around with his much younger wife, *but don't they all?* she thought. *Second and third wives are hardly ever age-appropriate for men like him.*

Once a well-respected businessman in his own right, Winfred Fisk took a hit in the crash of 2008 and was forced into long-overdue retirement. Kay felt sorry for her grandfather most of the time . . . put out to pasture and stubbornly refusing to accept it.

"Ugh, not him too," MaryJo said, looking down the aisle at the church's latest arrival. "I really cannot deal with him right now."

"Who?" asked Ryan.

"Him," she repeated, nodding her head in the direction of a very well-dressed, distinguished-looking older gentleman walking their way. "Uncle Edward."

"I didn't know I had an Uncle Edward."

"He's our great-uncle," Kay clarified. "Dad's dad's brother. He's lived in London for the past forever."

"And thinks he's better than all of us because of it," MaryJo added, taking a deep breath to brace herself for his arrival.

"Uncle Edward," she smiled when he was a few feet away. "How nice of you to come all this way."

When their mom stepped out of earshot, Kay leaned over to whisper to her brother. "I always liked him, actually. I spent several weeks at his house in London one summer during college."

"So why does Mom hate him?" Ryan whispered back.

"Dad told me once that his family didn't all approve of Mom. They – well, Grandpa at least – thought Mom was a gold digger. I think she's had a chip on her shoulder ever since." Kay looked up and saw the ushers motioning for everyone to take their seats. "C'mon. It's starting."

****

When the several hundred guests had squeezed into the pews of St. Monica's Church, Father Gerry walked up to the lectern and turned to face the crowd.

"Good afternoon. I'd like to welcome you all to what I hope will be a celebration of life. I've known of Tom Wilson the business titan for a long time, and I met Tom Wilson the philanthropist and occasional penitent several years ago, but it was only recently that I had the privilege to get to know Tom Wilson the person. The husband, the father, the grandfather, the friend. The child of God. And it is from those moments, seated in my office or having coffee across the street, that I know Tom does not want us to be sad today.

"He told me once," the pastor continued, "'Padre, I'm only here on Earth for a short period of time. Even if I live to 100, that's still a blip on the radar of history. So I'm okay if people don't remember me. If I don't have some huge legacy.' He said, 'what I want to do is create organizations and inspire people to continue to do good deeds long after I'm gone and forgotten'."

Father Gerry paused and scanned the crowd. "Think on that for a moment. Here was a man of immense wealth, power, and prestige, but he didn't spend his time thinking only of himself. He turned his attention to helping others and how he could do so in the most impactful way possible." The priest smiled. "To me, that attitude in and of itself is quite the legacy. A legacy I see in the Wilson After-School Program here at St. Monica's. In the Wilson Pediatrics Wing at Mount Sinai Hospital. A legacy I see most clearly in the hearts and minds of his children.

"Of course," Father Gerry added, "everyone here also knows that Tom Wilson wasn't perfect."

A few grumbles filled the sanctuary.

"None of us are. Tom was a perfectionist, though. Extremely competitive. Long to remember and sometimes slow to forgive. And those are just the things he would admit to me!"

Laughter replaced the earlier discontent in the pews.

"But you all wouldn't be here today to remember a bad man. Tom Wilson was a good man. A devoted husband, loving father and grandfather, gifted businessman, and generous philanthropist. And, I venture to add, a success in his goal to leave a legacy that will far outpace his life.

"One member of that legacy, his son Tripp, will now say a few words."

THIRTY-SEVEN

Tripp Wilson stood up from the front row, buttoned his suit jacket, and walked to the lectern in the front of the sanctuary.

Being the oldest child of the deceased, Tripp was selected to speak on behalf of the family. Reaching inside his jacket pocket, he pulled out his speech, unfolded the paper, and placed it on the pulpit.

Tripp took a deep breath. *Why couldn't Kay do this? She's better at shit like this than me.* He paused. *Man up, Tripp. Do it for Dad.*

"Fathers aren't supposed to die," he began.

"A father, to a son, is a giant of a figure," Tripp continued. "All-knowing, all-powerful . . . invincible. The thing about my father is that he wasn't only a giant to me. He was *the* Tom Wilson. All-knowing, all-powerful, and invincible to the entire city.

"When I was a boy, in my eyes, my dad was less of a parent and more of a god. Sorry Father," Tripp added, and muffled laughter rippled through the cathedral. "It wasn't until I got older that I really began to know my father the man. He was still hard-working; still brilliant. He modeled a love for family that I've tried to emulate with my own wife and our unborn child. My father was, in short, everything I wanted and still want to be." He paused. "The only thing he wasn't, in the end, was invincible." The younger Thomas Wilson sighed and shook his head. "None of us are."

Tripp ran his hand through his hair, a gesture that many in the audience recognized as something his father would also do. "I've been thinking these past several days about the best way to say goodbye. I decided – I'm not. We don't say goodbye to Thomas Wilson II because he lives on. He lives on in his wife, his two sons, his daughter, his grandchildren, his business, the many charities he founded or funded, and the friends who have gathered here today to remember him.

"I won't say goodbye. But I will say thank you."

Tripp looked over at the casket. "Thank you, Dad, for making me who I am. I promise I won't let you down."

There wasn't a dry eye in the house when Tripp stepped down from the lectern and returned to his seat.

****

After the deceased's family, friends, and fans departed the church – some of them headed to the burial site in Westchester County, others on their way home – Dennis lingered behind.

"Excuse me, Father?" he asked when Gerry Napier was finished with his memorial service duties.

"Yes?"

"I'm Detective Van Hatcher. NYPD."

"Oh, Detective. Nice to meet you," the priest replied. "I met your boss earlier, the commissioner."

Dennis nodded his head. "Yes sir. He and Mr. Wilson were close friends."

"They were, yes." Father Gerry paused. "Is there something I can do for you?"

"Do you have a minute to talk? Are you not going to the cemetery?"

Gerry shook his head. "They're not doing any kind of graveside service. Tom didn't specify and Mrs. Wilson preferred it this way. Why don't we walk back to my office?" the priest suggested. "We can talk in private."

"You mentioned in the eulogy that you and Tom talked here in your office. About what?"

"You should know better than that, Detective. Seal of the Confessional – I can't tell you anything that Tom Wilson told me in confidence."

"Okay. I get it," Dennis said with a nod. "Hopefully you can still help me, though."

"I'll try."

"When did Wilson start coming here?"

"Umm, late May. Early June, maybe."

"Do you know what prompted the sudden surge of faith?"

"Can't answer that."

"Given what you know and are allowed to say, do you think suicide is a possibility?"

Gerry Napier leaned back in his chair and linked his fingers behind his head. "Possible? Yes. Anything is possible. Probable? I would say no. Tom was looking forward to the future, as far as I could tell. He was haunted by the past, to be sure, but looking forward to the future."

"And you won't tell me why he was haunted by his past?"

"That's correct. I won't."

"Did you ever see him talking to other people?" Dennis asked. "Arguing on the phone or anything like that?"

"No. He always came alone. Worshipped alone. Today is the first time I met his family."

"Did anyone ever approach you about Mr. Wilson? Ask questions about why he was meeting with you?"

The priest shook his head. "Tom was a ghost in this parish. Came and went unnoticed. He seemed to like it that way."

"If things change, or you think of anything, here's my number," said Dennis, passing his business card to Father Gerry. "Call me anytime."

THIRTY-EIGHT

McSorley's in 20?

The text message popped up on Vanessa's phone at the 5th Precinct.

Sure, she replied. See you there.

Detective Smith locked her computer, tossed her cell phone in her purse, and walked north on Elizabeth Street toward the pub that often served as her and Dennis' second office. She passed through Chinatown into the East Village and arrived at McSorley's Old Ale House.

Founded in 1854 as a 'no girls allowed' pub, McSorley's was famous for only serving two kinds of beer (light and dark) and for being a popular hangout for New York City's men and women in uniform.

"Can't we pick somewhere quieter every once in a while?" asked Vanessa, making a face as she scanned the bar full of police officers and firemen stopping by after their shifts. *Not to mention women on the hunt for a man in uniform*, she thought.

Dennis shook his head. "Nope. I know it may not be your scene, Smith, but coming here and socializing will do as much for your career as a whole string of collars could."

"How will stomping around on sawdust-covered floors help my career as much as arresting criminals?"

Van Hatcher smiled at his partner, remembering himself at her age. "The department is a fraternity, right?"

"Yeah."

"Okay, well that means that once you reach a certain level, it becomes who you know in addition to what you know. Guys don't wanna work for somebody they don't know or don't trust. Believe me, trust is built in places like McSorley's."

Vanessa sighed, knowing that Dennis was right. And that she was lucky to be partnered with the NYPD's best detective. *That still doesn't change the fact that this bar is not my style. At all.*

Putting aside her thoughts, Vanessa looked across the table at her partner. "So, how was the funeral?"

"I didn't learn much, except that Tom Wilson was even more of a rock star than we thought. I don't think either of his sons could've done it. The teenager looked like his world had fallen apart, and Tripp stood to lose too much if his dad died. You should've heard his eulogy. Very impressive."

"Do you think the daughter could've done it?"

"I dunno. She's a mystery. If I had to guess, if we're going with murder – rather than an accident or suicide – my money's still on the son-in-law. Motive, opportunity, and a generally grumpy disposition."

Vanessa laughed. "Oh yeah, I can see that theory going over really well in court. 'What, in your professional opinion, made Mr. Eckersely the prime suspect?' 'Well, your honor, he was really grumpy'."

Dennis tossed a french fry at his partner's head. "You know what I meant."

"I know, I know. And I agree – if anybody's our guy, I think he is. That's a big, fat inheritance coming his wife's way. But we've gotta be able to prove him guilty before we confront him."

Van Hatcher nodded in agreement. "Print off copies of those bank statements we pulled up. I want to be able to show Eckersely that we're not bullshitting him. Maybe that will keep him from bullshitting us. At the very least, if we catch him in a lie about any of it, we can dangle a false statements or obstruction charge over his head to get him to talk."

THIRTY-NINE

Not wanting the witness/suspects to be able to talk to each other and corroborate their stories, the detectives scheduled all three of the victim's children – Tripp, Kay, and Ryan – for back-to-back-to-back interviews the next day.

Citing a busy work schedule that afternoon, Tripp came in first.

"Thanks for taking the time," Dennis said as his suspect sat down in a metal chair in the witness box. "I heard your speech at the funeral, by the way. Very moving."

"Thank you," Tripp answered, his chair screeching against the floor as he scooted closer to the table. "I was trying to make him proud. To do justice to the kind of man he was, you know?"

"I do. And you did."

"How about you help us get justice for his life?" asked Vanessa.

Tripp nodded his head. "Absolutely. Yes. Whatever you need."

"According to everyone else's accounts," Detective Smith began, "you were the last person to see your father alive."

"Yeah. I was." Tripp paused. "It really hits you when you hear somebody say it like that. 'To see him alive'." The thirty-five year old leaned back in his chair and stared at the far corner of the ceiling. After a few seconds, he shook his head as if to jolt himself back to the present. "Sorry. Ask away. Like I said, whatever you want to know."

"What happened that night?"

Tripp looked at the detectives in confusion. "Aren't you trying to figure that out for us?"

"No, I meant earlier in the night. Leading up to your father's disappearance."

"Oh. Right. Umm . . . well, we spent the day at sea.

Swimming, laying out on the deck. Took the jet skis out for a little while. Ryan and Luke wanted to waterski."

"On jet skis?"

"Yeah, you attach a tow rope to the back. The engines on those things are so powerful now that they can easily pull a skier. But anyway, that's not important. Umm . . . what else? We pulled Mom and Madison around on an inner tube a couple times."

Tripp paused and a distant smile crossed his face. "It was a good day."

"Then what happened?"

"We ate dinner on Staniel Cay. It's a small resort in The Exumas."

"We know. We went there."

"Oh, right. After dinner everybody went their separate ways to go to sleep. Dad invited me up to the top deck for our usual nightcap."

"Only you?"

"No, Ryan came too. He just had a splash," Tripp added.

"Was anybody else there?"

"No. Only the three of us. Dad asked Luke too, but he always said no."

"What'd you drink?" asked Dennis.

"Same thing we drank every night. Whisky."

"What'd you talk about?"

"Nothing really. Ryan's upcoming tennis season. How you can't see a sky like that in Manhattan."

"That was all?" Vanessa asked.

"Pretty much. Ryan drank a couple sips, I finished my glass, and we called it a night."

"Did your father do the same?"

Tripp shook his head. "He said he was going to stay up there a little longer, which he usually did. I think he liked the quiet." *And the extra booze*, Tripp thought, but didn't say so.

"Were you aware that your father was taking a prescription sleep aid?"

"I know he took Ambien sometimes. Or at least he said he did."

"What about mixing the two – Ambien and alcohol?"

Tripp sighed. "Dad drank a lot these past few months. Pretty much everything he took would've been mixed with alcohol."

"Even at work?"

"No, he wouldn't risk the company like that. Wilson|Cole was his first love and his favorite child. No . . . but nights and weekends were fair game."

"Any idea why?" Vanessa asked. "Why the sudden increase?"

Tripp shrugged his shoulders. "I don't know. None of us knew."

Dennis pulled a piece of paper from the folder in front of him and placed it on top of his notes. "Maybe you can shine a light on something else for us, Tripp. There were a couple of charges on your credit card bill that stood out as being, well, we'll call them interesting."

"Okay," Tripp said, shifting in his chair. "Which charges?"

"The Avery Firm."

"It's a private investigator."

"Suspicious about something?"

"Interested," Tripp replied. "For the past few years, I've been making some investments on my own. Nothing big. Just getting my feet wet in case I ever want to go solo. It can get kinda stifling in a family business, you know?"

"Most people don't hire a private investigator before they make a financial investment," Dennis pointed out.

"It's not a normal investment. There are a few buildings for sale in and around Purchase, the town where I live. I'm thinking of buying one so Anya can expand her store. She's always talking about how she'd like to make some of the clothes in-house."

"And the P.I. was to find out more information about

134

those properties?"

"The properties, the owners, the neighborhoods. I don't want to buy some place and a month later find out that it was a secret gang hideout or something."

"What about the fertility clinic charge?" asked Vanessa. "Six hundred dollars to a Dr. Johnson?"

"Whatever happened to my medical privacy?"

Interesting, Dennis thought. *He has to know that answer makes him look suspicious.* "Don't need privacy if you have nothing to hide," he commented.

Tripp laughed. "So says the police detective. I'm pretty sure the Bill of Rights reads differently."

"This isn't the time or place to get into a debate about constitutional rights to privacy," Vanessa said. "Look, Mr. Wilson, if you tell us that you have some physical condition that needed treatment, then we'll drop it. You're right – there are privacy laws surrounding your medical records. I only brought it up because Dr. Johnson is a fertility specialist. Most people who are considering things like IVF will make more than one trip to the clinic. It's suspicious because you only went once."

Tripp nodded his head. "Okay. I get that. Not that it's any of your business, but to show you that I don't have anything to hide, I'll tell you. Anya and I were having trouble getting pregnant. I thought maybe it was my fault. I went to the clinic to get tested, but everything came up fine. She's almost four months pregnant now." He smiled. "Sometimes it just takes a little while."

FORTY

Next up in the Fifth Precinct's witness box was Ryan Wilson, Tom and MaryJo's youngest. Wearing sneakers, pressed khakis, and a 'St. George's Tennis' t-shirt, Ryan was a prototypical Mid-Atlantic prepster.

Sitting across from the teenager, Detective Van Hatcher looked at his notes from the day's earlier interview. He wanted to make sure that the suspects' stories all matched. *But not too well*, he thought. *Nothing in a murder investigation ever wraps up neat and tidy. If it does*, Dennis knew, *somebody's lying.*

"So, Ryan, tell us about the last day on the boat."

"The last day?"

"Yes."

"Well, I had stayed up late watching a movie, so I slept in the next morning. Or at least I planned to. At around seven or so, Tripp busted into my room and shook me until I woke up."

"Wait," Vanessa cut in, "which day is this?"

"The last day on the boat. After my dad went missing."

"Oh, I meant the day before that when your father was still there. But this is good. Keep going."

"Okay, well, like I said, Tripp woke me up and started yelling 'where's Dad', 'have you seen Dad', 'we can't find Dad' . . . stuff like that."

"What did you think?" asked Vanessa.

"At first I thought I was dreaming. Cuz I went to sleep like four hours earlier. But he kept yelling at me and wouldn't leave so I sat up and was like 'what do you mean where's Dad?'"

"And that's how you found out your father was missing."

The teenager nodded his head.

"What happened next?"

"I got up and started looking for him, obviously. We checked all of the rooms and bathrooms. Was the dinghy still there? What about the jet skis? All of that. Trying to think of any reason why he wouldn't be there."

"Was everyone helping in the search?" asked Dennis.

Ryan nodded. "Of course. I mean, not Maddy or Harper. But everybody else. Ship called the Coast Guard like immediately, even before the rest of us had checked the whole boat."

"Was anyone acting out of the ordinary? Too calm or too upset?"

Ryan cut his eyes over at the detectives. "How could somebody be too upset about my dad disappearing?"

"You know – hysterics, over-the-top type stuff?"

"My mom was a wreck," Ryan remembered, "but why wouldn't she be?" He paused. "I guess I still don't understand the question."

"Don't worry about it," Van Hatcher replied. "What about the rest of the trip before your dad disappeared? Was anyone acting strangely? Out of the ordinary?"

The boy shook his head and looked down at the table. "Nah. Everything seemed normal. Except for Dad's drinking, but that had kinda become a new normal for us." Ryan sighed and raised his eyes up to look at the detectives. "Did he really O.D. on alcohol and sleeping pills?"

"Who told you that?"

"My mom."

Dennis let out a deep breath. *I hate it when they're all close like this and can talk to each other between interviews.* "We don't know," he replied.

"Oh." Ryan tapped his fingers on the metal table, a nervous habit filling the room with its *bah da dum* rhythm. "The crazy part is," he continued, "we were gonna do the intervention on that trip."

Vanessa looked up from her notebook. "What intervention?"

137

Bah da dum.

Bah da dum.

"Our intervention with Dad. We got together with Mom our the first day on *The Arvid* –"

"Who is we?" Dennis asked.

Bah da dum.

"Tripp, Kay, and me. We said we were worried about Dad's drinking and wanted to stage an intervention." *Bah da dum.* "We wanted to have it on the boat so he couldn't run away from it."

Nobody else has mentioned this, Dennis thought, double-checking his notes to make sure.

"Did your father know about this planned meeting?"

Ryan shook his head and frowned. *Bah da dum.* "Don't think so." *Bah da dum.*

"Is there anything else you remember from the trip? Anything you think might be important?"

The victim's youngest child thought for a minute, still drumming his fingers. "No." *Bah da dum.* "I don't think so."

"How about your relationship with your dad?" Dennis asked. "Good? Bad? Other? Was he annoying you being all up in your grill about school?"

Ryan looked over at Vanessa in confusion.

She smiled. "He tries to be cool sometimes. Just ignore it."

The teenager nodded. "Gotcha. And no. Dad was great. The best," he said, pain entering his voice.

"What about everybody else in the family? Were there any fights during the cruise?"

Ba da dum.

"Kay and Luke didn't seem too happy," Ryan remembered, leaning back and shoving his hands in his pockets. "But Luke never seems happy. He's so WAF."

"He's so what?"

"WAF. Long A . . . rhymes with faith. Well, sort of. Anyway: weird as fuck. WAF."

Vanessa laughed and her partner rolled his eyes.

"Was he WAFer than usual on the trip?" asked Dennis.

"What?"

"Weirder," Smith translated.

Ryan looked at Dennis like the older man had three heads. "There's no WAFer. It's not a cookie. It's just WAF."

"Did anything about his behavior seem out of the ordinary?" Van Hatcher asked, giving up after his two failed attempts at teenage slang.

"No. Not that I can remember."

"If anything does come to mind," Vanessa said, "give us a call. Or text. You can even message us on Twitter. @NYPD5Pct."

FORTY-ONE

Kay Wilson Eckersely arrived shortly after her younger brother left.

Detective Smith could tell by the way the other woman walked that she was going to be trouble. *Here comes Miss Thing*, she thought. *Strutting in here like she owns the place.*

Kay's stiletto heels click-clacked on the hardwood floor of the 5th Precinct, turning heads and drawing glares for the disruption.

"Right this way, Mrs. Eckersely," Dennis said. If he was annoyed by the suspect's attitude, he didn't show it.

'You can't be a good detective if you don't have a good poker face', Vanessa thought, repeating one of her partner's favorite lines. *Seriously, though – her outfit, including the purse, has to cost upwards of $1,000. Who wears that to a police station?*

Kay placed her oversized handbag on the metal table in the witness box and eyed the chair behind her. "Can I stay standing?" she asked. "These pants are Saint Laurent. They'll stain."

"Sit," Dennis commanded.

Kay rolled her eyes but did as she was told. "Listen, Detectives, I know you have a job to do and I – we all – very much appreciate your doing it. But you really need to back off of my mom."

"Excuse me?"

"She's a mess. She's always been a rock; my whole life she's been this calm, steady presence. But if you could've seen her this past week . . ." Kay's words broke off and she shook her head. "She's a mess. An absolute wreck. The best actress in the world couldn't fake the kind of pain and grief she's feeling. Maybe somebody did kill my dad. I don't know. What I do know is that, whatever happened – if anything – my mom had nothing to do with it. So back off, alright?"

Van Hatcher smiled. "I'm sorry, Mrs. Eckersely. There must have been some confusion. You seem to think that you've gone to a day at the spa."

"What?"

"This is a police station," he explained. "I am a police detective. You are a witness in a murder investigation. You sit when told to sit. You answer when told to answer. And you will not, under any circumstances, tell me or my partner how to do our jobs. Are we clear?"

Kay shrunk down in her chair. "Uh-huh."

"I'm sorry, I couldn't hear you."

"Yes. We're clear."

"Good. Now, Detective Smith, I believe you had some questions ready to go."

Vanessa opened the folder in front of her and picked up a pen to write down notes.

"You're aware that we already talked to your brothers, correct?"

Kay nodded her head.

"And you're aware that there's no such thing as a little white lie when it comes to police questioning, correct?"

"I'm not stupid, Detective."

"Alright, then you should be able to tell me about the inheritance you're set to receive from your dad's estate. It's a considerable sum, no?"

"I think so. At least that's what Mom has said."

"That money will go a long way toward paying off some of your debts," Vanessa suggested.

"I . . . I don't know what you're talking about."

"No?"

The socialite confidently shook her head.

Her eyes tell a different story, though, Vanessa noticed.

"You can feign ignorance, ma'am," Dennis said, "but we know quite a bit. How your husband took out a second mortgage on your house. How last year you sold all of your cars and converted to leased hybrids under the guise of wanting to be eco-friendly. How you never invite people to your home because you don't want them to know you fired your housekeeper six months ago. How your daughters are now on an installment payment plan at their school."

"Okay, okay," Kay replied, holding up her hands. "I get it."

"Just a couple more," the detective said. "We also know that your 'volunteer' position at the art gallery is actually paid."

"And that you and your husband have credit card debt in excess of $300,000," Vanessa added.

Kay slumped back in her chair and let out a deep breath. "Is there a point to this?" she asked. When the detectives didn't respond, she said: "okay, yes, it's true. We're broke. Luke has a gambling problem. I keep telling him to get help before he ruins all of our lives, but he won't listen. The last time I checked, though, it wasn't a crime to be in debt."

"That's true, it's not. But it is a crime to kill someone in order to collect your inheritance."

"What?!" Kay stood up so fast that her chair flew into the wall. "You can't seriously – I mean there's no way – he was *my dad*!"

Detective Van Hatcher stood and walked around the table, stooping down to pick up the chair.

"Sit."

Kay stared at him with a mixture of anger and shock. Reluctantly, she followed orders and sat down.

"You can understand, ma'am, why we would question you," Vanessa said, resuming the interview.

Kay cut her eyes over at Detective Smith and looked her up and down in disapproval. *She can't be any older than I am*, Kay thought. *In her cheap, off-the-rack, washing machine safe suit.* Sitting up tall, she adopted the same aristocratic air that had been bred into her family for centuries.

"Actually," she said, "I don't understand. I already told the police in the Bahamas everything I know. When I went to sleep, my father was alive. When I woke up, he was missing. The girls were in bed with me all night. Ask Madison. She'll tell you that I never left.

"My life has been completely shattered by all of this, and to think that you now suspect I would be capable of *murdering* my own father?" Kay huffed in disgust. "I didn't do it and I don't know who did. If anyone. May I please leave now?"

She didn't wait for a response before standing up and walking toward the door.

"Yes," Dennis said, "you're free to leave. But don't go far, understand?"

Kay's only reply was to glare at the detectives before stalking out of the interrogation room.

Dennis and Vanessa stood in the doorway, watching their suspect sashay her way through the precinct.

"Whatcha think?" Vanessa asked. "Do you trust her?"

"Not as far as I could throw her. I bet the husband's in on it too. Get him in here. Let's nail the bastards."

FORTY-TWO

"Is Eckersely on his way in?" Dennis asked later that afternoon.

Vanessa, seated at her desk, held up her index finger and pointed at the phone pressed against her ear.

"Are you sure?" she asked. "Can you send me that documentation? Okay, great. Thank you."

Setting down the receiver, Vanessa turned to face her partner. "Luke Eckersely didn't kill his father-in-law."

"What makes you say that – and with such confidence no less?"

"I was on the phone with the organizer of an elite internet gambling community," Detective Smith replied. "High-dollar buy-ins. Serious gamblers only."

"Sounds like Luke's kind of set-up."

"It is. He's one of their regulars. I called him to schedule an interview and he said he had an alibi. On the night Tom Wilson disappeared, Luke was online and actively participating in a poker game."

"Being logged in doesn't mean he was sitting in front of his computer the whole time."

Vanessa shook her head. "They don't just sign on to play. They use a secure video conference feed to make sure everyone is who they say they are and nobody is cheating."

"So all of his fellow gamblers saw our murder suspect continuously that night for . . ."

"Eight and a half hours."

Dennis whistled. "That's quite a game. But what about breaks? Surely they didn't all sit there for eight hours with no trips to bathroom or anything."

"I asked about that," Vanessa replied. "The organizer said they're really strict about leaving your spot for any reason. With the amount of money they're playing for, they're all paranoid about someone gaining an unfair advantage. If you have to use the restroom or need to leave the video conference for any reason, you're timed. Ninety seconds max or you're kicked out of the game and lose any money you've put into it. He said a lot of players will carry their laptop or tablet with them wherever they go so they don't risk running over the ninety seconds."

"Shit. Ninety seconds wouldn't be long enough to go up to the top deck, kill Tom, and get back to his room." Dennis paused. "Eckersely is clean. Shit. Back to square one."

FORTY-THREE

The next morning, in the basement of the 5th Precinct, the medical examiner was in her office reading the results of the DNA tests she ordered on Tom Wilson and his family. Commissioner Clark had declared that no stone be left unturned, and Dr. Templeton wanted to ensure that the victim didn't die of a genetic disorder. Also, if he did, she wanted to be able to warn his children about their own risk.

Even with a call from the commissioner's office to speed things up, the specialized tests still took a couple of weeks.

Dr. Templeton scanned the results and furrowed her brow. *That doesn't make any sense*, she thought.

A knock at the door made the M.E. jump.

"Oh, Mrs. Wilson, it's you. Perfect timing. Come on in."

"Thank you for agreeing to meet with me," MaryJo said. "I know I'm probably supposed to go through the detectives, but all I keep hearing from them is 'we don't know' and 'we're working on it'. I want to know how my husband died. I know you haven't figured out who killed him, if anyone, but I want to know how. I want to understand what he went through."

The medical examiner sighed. "To be perfectly honest with you, ma'am, I don't think we'll ever know with any degree of certainty what killed your husband. The night he died, his blood alcohol level was high enough to cause significant mental, physical, and sensory impairment. He took more than the recommended dosage of Ambien. And I found seawater in his lungs, telling me that he could've drowned."

"Thomas was an excellent swimmer."

"No one is a good swimmer when they're that drunk," Dr. Templeton replied. "We also know that he had a heart attack. Cause of death could've been any one or a combination of all four: alcohol poisoning, overdose, drowning, or heart attack."

"And you can't figure out which it was?"

"I'm afraid not, ma'am. Not on the basis of an autopsy alone. Detectives Van Hatcher and Smith may uncover something, but from my angle it's very uncertain. I'm glad you came in today, though," the M.E. continued. "I received the results of the DNA tests that I ran to look for genetic abnormalities."

"Did it help you with the case?" MaryJo asked hopefully.

"No, but I do have a question for you. Was Ryan adopted?"

"No."

"That's really strange, then. His blood type doesn't match. You're A-Positive. Your husband was also A-Positive. Ryan is B-Negative."

MaryJo's face turned pale and she spun around in her chair to make sure no one was listening behind her. *Shit*, she thought. *Shit shit shit*. The widow looked down at her hands and twisted her wedding ring back and forth on her finger. Finally, Mrs. Wilson let out a deep sigh. Years of pain, guilt, and embarrassment flowed with it.

"Thomas didn't know," she explained. "Never even suspected it, as far as I could tell. Things in that department had slowed down a lot by then, but there was always a time every month or so when he was so drunk I could've told him that the pope stopped by the night before and he'd believe me. Convincing him that we made love and Ryan was an 'oopsie baby' was simple."

MaryJo shook her head and pinched the bridge of her nose. "He was an 'oopsie baby', that part is true. Just not with my husband."

The medical examiner sat across from MaryJo with her eyebrows raised and jaw dropped.

"Listen, Mrs. Wilson, I'm not a priest or a lawyer or a psychiatrist. There's no confidentiality here."

"I know," MaryJo said with a nod as tears filled her eyes. "I know. I guess . . . well, I guess I thought if I told you the truth then you'd find a way to leave all of this out of your report."

"Mr. Wilson's blood type is a standard inclusion, but I suppose there's no need to list the blood types of his children. All I really have to say is that I didn't detect any genetic irregularities that could've explained his death."

MaryJo smiled through her tears. "Thank you. Thank you very much."

"Umm, if I may . . . does the real father know?"

"I think he might suspect it. But he's never asked. And I've never told."

The M.E. shook her head. "I couldn't do that. I'd want to know for sure one way or the other."

MaryJo stood up from her chair and regained her composure. "Yes, well, you'd think differently if you knew the whole story." *And if finding out the truth would destroy not only your marriage but also your billion dollar business partnership*, she thought.

"Thank you for your time, Doctor," said Mrs. Wilson, reaching out to shake hands. "And your discretion."

****

Five miles north of Chinatown and unaware of the conversation happening in the basement of their precinct, Detectives Van Hatcher and Smith were ushered into the spacious corner office of Charles Cole, Tom's partner and co-founder of their investment firm. Wilson|Cole was located adjacent to Bryant Park in the heart of Midtown Manhattan.

"Fancy," Vanessa whispered.

"The rent on a closet in this building is probably more than my entire apartment," Dennis replied.

"That's because your building is rent-controlled. Lucky bastard. Remind me again why we're interviewing this guy?"

148

"He's Tom Wilson's business partner and one of his oldest friends."

"But he wasn't on the boat."

"Doesn't mean he won't know something that could help us," Dennis replied.

Charles Cole picked that moment to stride into his office. Sixty-four years old and in great shape, with smooth silver hair and a megawatt smile, Charles would've been the crush-worthy boss in the building if not for the devilishly handsome good looks of his business partner.

"Sorry I'm late," he said, motioning for the detectives to sit down in the chairs beside his desk. "I was having breakfast with my wife and mother-in-law. Our waiter obviously didn't know that, in this city, time is money."

"No problem," said Dennis. "I'm Detective Van Hatcher. This is my partner, Detective Smith. Thank you for taking some of that valuable time to meet with us."

"Of course. Anything for Tom. I've known him since freshman year of college – did you know that?" Charles sighed. "I still can't believe he's gone."

"Maybe you can help us out," Dennis said. "We're coming up empty on our leads. Anything you know, even if you think it's not important, tell us."

Charles leaned forward, placing his elbows on his desk and interlocking his fingers. "I'm not sure what I could tell you that you wouldn't already know, but I'll try."

"Was there any trouble at home?" asked Vanessa.

Charles flinched. "Me or Tom?"

"Well . . . I meant Tom."

"Ah," he replied, nodding his head. "Sorry."

"You're having trouble at home?" Dennis asked.

Trouble at home leads to stress at work which leads to a fight with his partner, the detective thought. *Maybe Cole is a suspect after all.*

Charles shrugged. "Carolyn and I have never had what you would call a happy marriage. My father and hers were

149

law partners. It was more or less arranged since we were born."

"And you find that missing happiness elsewhere?" Vanessa guessed.

He shrugged his shoulders again. "Have you ever seen the show 'House of Cards'? The American version with Kevin Spacey? How they love each other but they aren't faithful? Same thing – minus the murders, of course. Carolyn and I are a partnership. We get what we need from each other and don't mind if we get other things we need from other people. It works."

"Did she ever get what she needed from Tom Wilson?"

Charles jerked his head up in surprise. "What? No, never. Not that I wouldn't put it past her to try. But no. Tom wouldn't cheat. Didn't have it in him."

"Would MaryJo?"

The interview subject let out a deep sigh and leaned back in his chair, resting his hands in his lap.

Sonofabitch, Dennis thought. "I'd like to remind you that, even though you're not under arrest, making false statements to the police is a crime. And making false statements to intentionally impede an investigation is obstruction of justice."

Charles looked up at the detectives through hooded eyes. "It was a long time ago. Done and over with. We both knew it was a mistake. Tom never found out."

"Sonofabitch," said Vanessa, repeating her partner's thoughts.

"Mr. Wilson never found out as far as you know," Dennis surmised. "He could've learned about the affair, confronted MaryJo on the boat, and fallen overboard in a struggle. Could've found out and gotten depressed that his wife would cheat on him with his friend and business partner."

"That would explain the heavy drinking recently," Vanessa added.

"Sure would. Then a depressed Tom uses the yacht cruise as a convenient way to end his own life."

Charles Cole shook his head. "No. I've known Tom since we were both eighteen year old freshmen at Harvard. If he learned about MaryJo and me, I would've known."

"I bet he thought if his wife cheated on him with his business partner, he would've known," Vanessa muttered under her breath. Dennis bit back a smile.

"Come on, Mr. Cole. Help us out here. Otherwise I'm going to have no choice but to list you as a potential suspect."

"What? I wasn't even on the boat!"

Van Hatcher pursed his lips together into a frown. "Technicality. You had access to his office at work. Could've spiked his drink. His food. His medication. Lots of possibilities here, now that I know you're the kind of man who would sleep with his best friend's wife."

Cole set his jaw and glared at the detective. "I didn't do it. I wasn't there. I don't even know what kind of medication Tom was taking, if any. If you want a suspect, look at that damn son-in-law of his. Up to his eyeballs in debt and running around like a lunatic trying to keep it all a secret."

"Luke Eckersely was cleared," Vanessa said. "Alibi'd out. So did his wife. You can see her asleep on the bed in the background of the gambling video."

"So," Dennis said, "now you're the kind of man who sleeps with his best friend's wife and keeps secrets from that same friend when his daughter and granddaughters are in financial trouble."

"Fuck you, man," Charles replied, standing up from his chair. "I don't have to sit here and be attacked like this. I already told you what I know, which is nothing."

"Hold on a second, Mr. Cole," said Vanessa as the man walked toward the door. "I have one more question."

"What?"

"When was the affair between you and Mrs. Wilson?"

151

"What does it matter?"

"Humor me."

Cole shrugged his shoulders. "I don't know. Fifteen, sixteen years ago. Something like that. Now if you don't mind," he said, opening his office door, "I have work to do."

FORTY-FOUR

"Do you believe him?" Vanessa asked as they walked back to Dennis' car.

"About the affair? Absolutely."

"No, about the murder," she clarified. "Do you really think he doesn't know anything?"

"I do, actually. He's a piece of shit, but I think he's an innocent piece of shit." Dennis paused. "Why'd you want to know when the affair was?"

A spark entered Smith's eyes. "Ever notice how Ryan Wilson looks nothing like his brother and sister?"

"He looks like his mom."

"Meh . . . kinda. Reminds me more of a Cole than a Wilson."

Dennis nodded. "Tom finds out about the affair, puts two and two together about the kid, and stews over it for several months. When they get on the boat, he finally confronts his wife in a drunken rage."

"She fights back and he goes overboard."

"I think we need to pay a visit to the late Mr. Wilson's widow."

****

Twenty-two blocks north of Wilson|Cole, in Manhattan's tony Upper East Side, sat the elegant brownstone belonging to Tom and MaryJo. The mansion on East 63rd was five stories tall, six including the basement, and had four bedrooms, two kitchens, an elevator, an outdoor garden, and a rooftop terrace. Unlike many other NYC homes that were gutted and replaced with modern interiors, Tom and MaryJo preferred a traditional look with hardwood floors, original crown molding, and dark cherry woods for furniture and bookcases.

The exterior of the house was equipped with the latest security monitoring equipment, but it wasn't until after Tom's death that it started being used with any frequency. "I hate the idea of being spied on," he always said.

MaryJo, on the other hand, locked and alarmed herself in every chance she got. "There could be a murderer on the loose who is targeting my family," she told Alice Mason, the housekeeper. "I want that alarm on at all times."

Mrs. Mason and her husband lived in the basement. While Alice cooked and cleaned, Mark was the butler/handyman/family chauffeur. Tom had used a car service paid for by his company, but MaryJo would get Mark to drive her around the city. "It's so much easier than having to hail a cab."

"You should take an Uber, Mom," Ryan said while scrolling through Instagram on his phone. "Taxis are so five years ago."

Kay, who had come over to visit, laughed and rolled her eyes. "'So five years ago' when you were ten?"

Her teenage brother shrugged his shoulders. "Whatever. Uber is better."

"Not when I can have Mason take me," said MaryJo. "Private transport is always better than public."

"If you can afford it," Kay muttered.

"What?"

"Nothing." She leaned over to the coffee table and picked up a magazine to flip through. "Ugh, what the hell is wrong with people?" Kay said, throwing the magazine back down in disgust. "Can't they just leave us in peace?"

Ryan picked it up and flipped to the page Kay didn't like. There was a large picture of his mom leaving St. Monica's on the day of the funeral. "'Stylish and chic as always'," he read aloud, "'MaryJo Wilson wears her grief like it were a bespoke designer label'." He rolled his eyes and dropped the magazine. "What a bunch of little shits."

"Ryan!" MaryJo scolded.

"What? Kay said hell. Why can't I say shit?"

"Because you're fifteen. And I said so."

FORTY-FIVE

"I beg your pardon, ma'am," said Mr. Mason, standing in the doorway to the living room. "Two detectives from the NYPD are here to see you."

"Send them in, please."

Dennis and Vanessa arrived seconds later, escorted by the butler.

"That'll be all, Mason. Thank you." MaryJo smiled and extended her hand in greeting. "Welcome, detectives. Can I get you anything to drink?"

"No thank you," Dennis replied. "As I think I mentioned before, we're here to look around the house and your late husband's personal effects for any clues about what might have caused his death."

"Of course. How about I give you the grand tour? If you want to stop in any of the rooms as we go along, just let me know.

"We're on the first floor now," MaryJo said, "which has this room, obviously, and also a service kitchen and a garden out back. The second floor is the main kitchen and dining room. The top three floors are all bedrooms. Tom had a small home office on the third floor, right outside of our bedroom."

"We'll want to look around in there," said Vanessa.

Mrs. Wilson nodded her head and gestured toward the stairs. "Absolutely. This way."

Walking several feet behind their hostess, Detective Smith leaned over toward her partner. "This thing has six fireplaces," she whispered. "Who the hell needs six fireplaces?"

"Don't forget about the elevator," Dennis replied.

"Oh no, I like that. I would hate not having an elevator in my apartment building. I feel sorry for their dog, though," Vanessa said. "Only that tiny little yard in the back?"

"Are you kidding? That dog has the life. Most dogs in

the city don't have any yard at all, and their owners are gone at work all day. The Wilson dog has his own back yard, lives five blocks from Central Park, and his owner doesn't work. Plus there's a full-time, live-in housekeeper, so he's never left alone. Shit, I'd trade lives with that dog in a heartbeat."

Vanessa laughed. "Some might say it wouldn't be too much of a change for you."

"Huh?"

"Your reputation with the ladies for being a dog?"

"Oh," Dennis replied, rolling his eyes. "Whatever."

On the second floor of the house, a large walkway connected the kitchen with the dining room and served as a makeshift art gallery.

Vanessa, having studied art history in college, drooled at the masterpieces hanging from the walls.

That's a Rembrandt, she thought in awe. *There's another one. That's a Titian. Oh my gosh, there's a Caravaggio.* "Are these originals?" she asked.

"This hallway is," replied Kay, having joined the tour. "The rest are reproductions or works by lesser artists. Mom occasionally picks up an original by a master, though, and hangs them here."

"Your father wasn't a collector?"

Kay shook her head. "Not of art. He liked cars. And whisky. The wine collection's probably worth about 300 grand," she added in an almost off-hand manner.

"Where did he keep the cars?" Dennis asked. "There's not enough room here."

"Our house out in the Hamptons," MaryJo answered. "Under lock and key in a temperature-controlled garage."

"What did he have?"

"Don't know. Tripp could probably tell you. I'm sure Mason could as well."

"Oh wow," said Vanessa. "Is that what I think it is?"

The rest of the group followed her gaze to a large, mostly gold painting at the end of the hall.

157

"No, unfortunately that's not the original," MaryJo replied. "You've got a good eye, though. 'The Kiss' is one of Klimt's most famous paintings."

Following behind her mom, Kay shook her head. "I've always hated that thing," she whispered to Vanessa. "Looks like he's holding a decapitated head. Gave me nightmares as a kid."

Detective Smith smiled and glanced at the painting again. "I'm not really a Klimt fan either. Although I do like the Symbolist style, generally speaking."

"You know your art," Kay said with surprise.

Vanessa nodded. "I minored in art history in college. My parents told me to pick something useful for a major, so I did econ. But I loved my art history classes."

Continuing the tour, Dennis and Vanessa lingered for almost an hour in Tom's study. They looked through all of the drawers and cabinets but couldn't find anything.

"He didn't spend much time here," MaryJo explained. "All of his work files stayed at the office."

"Who's that one by?" asked Vanessa, pointing to a charcoal painting of a wine bottle. "I don't recognize the artist."

"Arvid," said Mary Jo. "It's the damndest thing. We bought the yacht, which was already named *The Arvid*, and then we discovered this painter named Arvid. And his first name Thomas, of all things. I thought it was neat and picked up a little one from a gallery."

Detective Van Hatcher looked over at the four-by-four original hanging on the wall. *She 'picked up a little one'*, he thought. *That thing probably cost more than my entire life savings.*

"Mrs. Wilson," Vanessa said as they climbed the stairs to the fourth floor. "I wondered if I might have a quick word in private."

"Certainly."

"While you ladies talk," said Dennis, "I think I'm going

to go see the butler. Mason, was it?"

MaryJo nodded. "Yes. Mark Mason. He should be around somewhere. Kay, why don't you see if you can help the detective find him?"

FORTY-SIX

Vanessa waited until the room was empty before beginning her questions.

"We met with your husband's business partner earlier today," she said.

"Charles?"

The detective nodded her head. "Unless there's another business partner we should know about?"

"No, only Charles. How's he doing? I haven't seen him since the funeral."

"Seemed fine to me. He did mention something, though, that I want to follow up on with you." Vanessa paused and looked to make sure Ryan and the housekeeper weren't listening. "Did you ever cheat on your husband, Mrs. Wilson?"

"Since you're asking, I'm going to assume Charles told you."

"*You* should've told us. Just like you should have told us about Ryan."

"How did you –"

"I called the medical examiner on the way over here to find out the results of the genetic testing. She told me about the blood types."

"So much for discretion."

"It looks very suspicious," Vanessa said. "Gives you a strong motive. And opportunity, since you and your husband slept in the same bedroom on the yacht."

"If I killed Thomas – which I did not – but if I had, and the police in the Bahamas ruled it an accident – which they did – why on earth would I ask Commissioner Clark to do his own investigation? If not for me, this would all be over. You and I never would have even met. But as things stand, there's a cloud hanging over everyone's lives and a hold on the insurance money."

"Nice way to cover your tracks."

Mrs. Wilson shook her head. "If I killed my husband, I'd be celebrating getting away with it, not asking the best detectives in the country to go sniffing around."

"I guess you have a point there, ma'am."

"Of course I have a point." She paused. "I'm going to assume that your suspecting me means you have no better leads? I heard that Luke had a gambling alibi, as sordid as that is."

"We're still working on it, Mrs. Wilson. It's a complicated case, but we're determined to find the truth."

****

Kay and Dennis found the butler in his workshop in the basement.

"I'm going back upstairs unless you need anything from me," she said.

"No, I think we'll be fine on our own," the detective replied.

After Kay left the room, Dennis sat down on a stool near a workbench and crossed his arms over his chest. "I've heard you called several things. Mason. Mr. Mason. Mark. Which do you prefer?"

"Mark's fine."

"Good. I'm Dennis."

The two men shook hands.

"I kind of felt like I was walking on eggshells up there," Dennis said, trying to build trust with the butler.

"It's a different world upstairs," Mark replied. "To be honest, I prefer the downstairs way of living."

"Why?"

"You've met them. Secrets, lies, addictions . . . and they're one of the best families in New York. Imagine what it's like with some of the more scandalous ones."

"Openly scandalous," Dennis corrected.

"Well, yeah. True." Mark shook his head. "There were a lot of skeletons in these closets before Mr. Wilson died. Now they're all starting to come out."

As expected, Dennis thought, *the butler knows all.* "Do you think any of those secrets got him killed?"

"Dunno. Maybe."

"Did Mr. Wilson ever confide in you? Share those secrets? Perhaps tell you what was bothering him so much the last few months of his life?"

"That's one thing I never could figure out. It wasn't my place to ask, and I never observed anything that would explain it. Mr. Wilson was always nice and friendly, but he clammed up this past summer. Became a different person."

"Do you mean his going to church?"

"And the drinking. Mostly the drinking. He started going through his liquor cabinet like it was a candy store. Downing the stuff like water." The butler shook his head. "Took to drinking a forty-year-old Dalmore Highlands single malt every night."

Upon seeing the detective's blank face, Mason added: "they're $3,500 per bottle. When he ran out of that, he bumped up to a forty-year-old Macallan that'll put you back a cool $8,500. I hid the really good stuff when I realized what he was doing. You know, the fifty-year Balvenies and Glendfiddiches."

Dennis nodded his head in feigned understanding. *He could've said he hid Mickey Mouse and Bugs Bunny and it would've meant as much to me.*

"I didn't have any doubt that he could afford it," the butler continued, "but that's a helluva expensive hobby to pick up. Especially every night and in your prime heart attack years." Mason crossed himself. "God rest his soul."

"Sounds like Mr. Wilson had a pretty serious drinking problem."

"Problem? Nah. He drank a lot, but I never heard him say 'I need a drink' or seem like he was addicted like an

162

alcoholic."

"So it was just a really expensive, what'd you call it? A hobby? A really expensive hobby that he happened to pick up a couple of months before his death?"

"Well, when you put it like that . . ." Mason paused. "It was almost as if, and I hate to use this word because of how he died, but it was like he was trying to drown out something else. Like he thought if he kept pouring whisky on it, eventually it'd go away."

"And Mr. Wilson never gave any hints about what that something was?"

"Nah. Nothing."

"Ok, thank you," Dennis replied, scribbling a few comments in the notebook he always kept in his back pocket. As he walked upstairs to find his partner, the detective still couldn't figure out Tom Wilson's behavior.

What are you hiding, old man? he wondered. *What are you hiding?*

FORTY-SEVEN

The NYPD's two best detectives got take-out Chinese food on the way back to their precinct in Lower Manhattan.

With a box of moo shu pork in one hand and a dry erase marker in the other, Van Hatcher sat in front of the whiteboard and looked at the case information. *Maybe if I stare long enough, something will come to me.*

Vanessa joined him a few minutes later, eating sweet and sour shrimp.

"Think Mrs. Mason would approve of our dinner choices?" she asked, referencing the Wilsons' housekeeper.

Dennis laughed. "I doubt it."

Detective Smith nodded in the direction of the whiteboard. "Figure it out yet?"

"I wish. I think if we can determine exactly where he was when he went overboard, then we'd have a better understanding of who could've snuck up there with him without being noticed."

"Do you have an extra marker?" Vanessa asked. "Mine's almost all gone."

"Yeah, check my desk."

Not finding any markers in the top drawer, Smith slid open the second one. Digging under papers to try to find something to write with, Vanessa saw a flat, navy blue box shoved in the far back of the drawer. On the top of the box was a bright green horizontal bar with twelve gold stars on it.

Glancing over her shoulder to make sure her partner wasn't looking, Vanessa took out the box and opened it.

"Holy crap."

"What?"

"This is a Medal of Honor."

Detective Van Hatcher walked over to his desk, took the box out of Vanessa's hand, and tossed it back in the drawer.

"I said you could look for a marker, not go on a

164

scavenger hunt. Here," Dennis added, "take my marker. We only need one."

"But . . . but that's a NYPD Medal of Honor," Vanessa said, pointing toward the desk. "The highest award a police officer can receive."

"So you've said. Come on. We've got a murder to solve."

Detective Smith crossed her arms and refused to move. "Not until you explain that medal."

Dennis shrugged his shoulders. "There's nothing to explain."

"Is it yours?"

"No, I stole it. Yes, of course it's mine."

"But you never said anything. We've been working together for four years and you've never told me about it."

Dennis let out a deep breath, realizing that his partner wasn't going to let him smooth talk his way out of this one.

"You never asked. And it happened a long time ago. Before you joined the force."

"What happened?"

"It was my first big case. I was assigned to a diamond heist. Tens of millions of dollars' worth of jewelry stolen from a private gallery. We figured out who the perp was, I tracked him down, caught him, and that was the end of it. Like I said," Dennis added, "no big deal. And of zero help to us on the Wilson case."

He turned to face the whiteboard. "If Tom Wilson was on the little side patio with somebody else and got into an argument," Dennis said, pointing at the floor plan of *The Arvid* that was taped to the board, "then the wife would've heard it. There's no way she wouldn't."

"Which points to him accidentally falling over," Vanessa replied.

"*If* he fell off the side patio."

"What?"

"Sorry," Dennis said, "but I realized we've been

operating on the assumption that he fell off that little ledge. It would actually make more sense if he went off the top or the back."

"Why? Mrs. Wilson said that her husband would go out on the patio at night."

"Eventually. He started the night on the top deck with Tripp and Ryan. And the top deck," Dennis said, pointing again, "is here. Toward the rear."

"Stern."

"What?"

"The back of a boat is the stern."

"Whatever. What I'm saying is, if he was super drunk and walked through the bedroom to get to the little patio, then no amount of NyQuil would've kept MaryJo from hearing him. Drunks can be a lot of things, but quiet isn't one of them. It seems much more likely that he would've fallen off the top deck."

Vanessa sighed. "How about this? We take the report, write on it 'who the hell knows', and call it a day? Front, side, back. Pushed, fell. Accident, murder." She ran her hands through her hair in frustration. "We've been at this for a solid three weeks, Dennis. And we still have nothing."

"Have a little patience," her partner counseled. "Have a little patience."

"Why aren't we focusing on the obvious?"

"Which would be?"

"His pre-death injury. The autopsy said that he had massive swelling and bruising in his groin area."

Dennis winced. "And?"

"And . . . what's one sure fire way to get a woman to kick you in the balls? Cheat on her."

"We don't know the killer was a woman."

"C'mon, you'd shoot a guy in the head before you'd kick him down there, wouldn't you?"

Dennis paused. "Yeah, probably. Guy code."

"Exactly," Vanessa said. "Tom has an affair, MaryJo

finds out about it, kicks him in the family jewels, and pushes him overboard."

Dennis scrunched his face in pain. "Can we please stop talking about groin kicking?"

"Okay. But you've gotta admit – it's a highly plausible theory."

Her partner shook his head. "Mrs. Wilson told us she went to bed at 10:30, and the younger son and daughter corroborated that."

"And what – nobody has ever left their room before? She could've easily snuck out without being noticed. The Nyquil could be a cover. You saw the floor plan for the yacht. The master is on a totally different level than the other bedrooms."

"True. I guess it's possible, sure. But Mrs. Wilson would never admit it and the kids would likely be in the dark about any affair." Dennis looked over at his partner and saw her eyes sparkling. *Uh oh*, he thought, *I know that look.*

"You know who might have the best chance of knowing?" Vanessa asked.

"The priest won't talk. Neither will the lawyer."

"No, no, not them. Commissioner Clark. Guys are even bigger gossips than girls. If our vic was having an affair, or was the kind of guy who might have an affair, his best friend and tennis partner would know."

Dennis sighed. *Yep. Crazy sparkle-eyed idea.* "You're out of your mind if you think I'm going to march into 1PP and ask the commissioner if his dead best friend was screwing around on his wife."

"Okay, fine. I'll do it."

FORTY-EIGHT

The earliest time that the commissioner had available was six o'clock the next evening, and even then it wasn't a full appointment.

"You've got twelve and a half minutes," Clark said when Dennis and Vanessa walked into his office. "Otherwise I'm going to be late for a meeting with the mayor."

Dennis elbowed his partner in the side, nudging her forward. *No way she's going to weasel out of being the one who asks him.*

"Umm, sir?" Vanessa said, wiping the palms of her hands on her pants. While Dennis was used to meeting one-on-one with Commissioner Clark, she wasn't. *And I have the sweat stains to prove it*, she thought.

"Yes?"

"We were hoping you could answer some questions about Tom Wilson."

"Sure. Shoot."

"Well, we're coming up empty on financial or other business motivations, and our main suspect – the son-in-law, Luke Eckersely – had an iron-clad alibi. I watched the video of him playing poker that entire night."

"Okay. What do you need from me?"

"You knew Mr. Wilson better than almost anybody. Do you think he was having an affair?"

"Tom? No way."

"Come on," Vanessa pressed, "a rich, handsome guy like that? I'm sure interns and associates and even Mrs. Wilson's friends were offering themselves up to him."

"Still doesn't mean he was the kind of guy who would step out on his wife," the commissioner replied. "I don't see it. He never did or said anything that would make me think he was cheating on MaryJo. Maybe he did. I don't know. But I don't see it happening." Clark paused. "Even if he had, I

168

don't think that would've caused his death. Tom was too careful . . . meticulous about everything. Dotted all the I's and crossed all the T's. He would've covered his tracks."

"What about the drinking, sir?" Dennis asked.

Derrick sighed. "Tom wasn't a cheater, but he wasn't a saint either. For as long as I've known him, he'd pick several nights a year and really let loose. He was a fun drunk, though. He'd drop his guard and sing and dance, and people loved him all the more for it. It showed that he was human rather than some Stepford machine.

"He was different the last couple months of his life, though," his friend continued. "Tom still held it together in public – the tabloids never picked up on anything. But he was different in private. Heavy drinking. A much more troubled outlook on the world."

"Did you ask him why?"

"He was my best friend. Of course I did."

"And?"

"He wouldn't tell me," the commissioner replied, thinking back to the last conversation he had with Tom.

~~~

"You sure that's a good idea?" Derrick asked, gesturing toward the bottle of scotch in Tom's right hand and the empty tumbler glass in his left.

"Don't you start too," Tom growled in reply. "MaryJo is on my case all the time about how I'm drinking too much."

Derrick leaned back in the leather chair in his home office and sighed. "Maybe that's because you are. I love you man, you know I do. But you're gonna kill yourself if you keep that up."

Wilson poured four fingers of Glenlivet into his glass and took a long sip, ignoring his friend's comment.

"At least tell me why," the commissioner said. "You've never been a big drinker before."

Tom drank another large gulp and paused, closing his eyes to feel the burn of the whisky as it traveled down his throat.

"You wouldn't understand," he finally replied.

"Try me."

Tom shook his head and flashed a smile. "Don't worry about it. Let's talk about something else, huh? How are your kids?"

~~~

In his office with the two detectives, Commissioner Clark ran a frustrated hand through his hair. "'Don't worry about it' was Tom's default answer for everything. Even back in college, if some kind of problem came up, he'd smile and tell me not to worry about it. It was the same with the drinking. I pressed him on it . . . the week before he left on the cruise I pressed him on it again. He just smiled that million dollar smile – or I guess with him that $200 million smile – and said I shouldn't worry about it." Derrick sighed. "Of course I did worry, but I'd known Tom long enough to know that he wasn't going to give me a straight answer."

"Do you think he could've killed himself?"

"He would've left a note. Tom hated loose ends. This investigation and uncertainty would've driven him crazy."

"Can I ask you one other thing, sir?" said Vanessa. "It's a bit off-topic."

"Sure, why not. The mayor's always running late anyway."

"I recently found Detective Van Hatcher's Medal of Honor in his desk drawer . . ."

Dennis glared at his partner. "That's completely irrelevant. I'm sorry, sir. We'll leave now."

"No, no, it's fine. What's your question, Smith?"

"Dennis tried to downplay the whole thing, kind of like he is now, and I couldn't find much information about it in

170

the system. But I did see that a Captain Derrick Clark was the one who recommended him for the award."

The commissioner looked at Dennis with a slight smile and shook his head. "In a drawer in your desk? Really?"

"I wear it when I'm expected to. What else am I supposed to do with it?"

"What happened?" Vanessa asked. "All he said was that he chased a diamond thief and arrested him. But that's not enough to get the Medal of Honor."

Again the commissioner smiled and shook his head. "She's too smart for you, Van Hatcher." Turning to the female detective, he said: "There's a little more to the story than that. It happened in December. Van Hatcher tracked the thief to a New York Waterway ferry. The guy saw Dennis on the boat with him and decided to make a break for it by jumping into the river. Van Hatcher followed suit. Jumped three stories from a moving ferry into the half-frozen Hudson. Your partner here started swimming after the suspect and the man opened fire, hitting Dennis in the shoulder. He returned fire, and they proceeded to have a James Bond-style underwater fight for both the firearms and the bag of diamonds."

"In the struggle, one of the guns went off and the bullet hit the perp in the head," Dennis said, finishing the story. "He sank to the bottom of the river while the diamonds and I went back to the surface."

"Holy crap."

"I was Van Hatcher's captain at the time," the commissioner said. "Don't take it personally, though. He's never liked to talk about it."

"Can't go around living in the past," Dennis replied.

Vanessa's cell phone started ringing. "I'm sorry, it's the medical examiner. I need to take this."

"She's gonna be a good one," Clark said after Smith left the room. "Great, even. Like you."

Dennis shook his head. "I hope not."

"You hope not? Why – don't want the competition?"

"Not that at all. In fact, I agree with you. Smith has a lot of potential. But to be truly great at this job, you have to give your life to it." Dennis paused. "She deserves better than that. So does her husband, by the way."

The commissioner looked across the desk at his best detective. "Don't look now, Van Hatcher, but I think you might actually be a halfway decent human being."

Dennis smiled and put his finger over his lips. "Shhh. You'll ruin my reputation with slander like that."

His boss laughed. "Get out of here. Go find me my murderer."

FORTY-NINE

After leaving police headquarters, Detective Van Hatcher took the Manhattan Bridge across the East River toward his apartment in Brooklyn. It was after eight o'clock and Dennis hadn't been home in three days, a combination of successful dates and a not-so-successful murder investigation.

Long hours and restless nights were nothing new to the veteran cop. Criminals didn't operate on a nine-to-five, Monday-to-Friday schedule, which meant that the NYPD didn't either. The job was particularly tough on detectives like Dennis. New crime scenes popped up at all hours, autopsies usually began every morning at 8am at the medical examiner's office, court testimony on prior cases could run days or even weeks, and witnesses and other persons of interest had to be brought in and questioned whenever they were found – *because we don't know how long it might take to find them again*, he thought.

Trudging up the stairs, Dennis unlocked the door to his apartment and was greeted by Murphy.

"Hey buddy, did you miss me?" he asked, scooping the fluffy cat into his arms. "I bet you did. I sure missed you," he added as Murphy rubbed his head under Dennis' chin and purred. "I think there's a Yankees game tonight. We should be able to catch most of it."

Dennis put Murphy back on the floor and walked into the kitchen to grab a beer from the refrigerator.

A second after he popped open the bottle, his doorbell rang.

"Geez," he sighed. "All I want is five minutes of silence. Five minutes to myself. Is that so much to ask, Murph?"

The cat, upon hearing visitors at the door, bolted for the safety of the bedroom.

Beer in hand, Dennis looked through the peephole and

saw his ex-wife and her twin daughters standing in the hall.

"What the –?"

He undid the bolt lock, lifted the chain, and pulled open the door.

"Jennifer. This is a surprise."

"I'm sorry," the former Mrs. Van Hatcher said with a grimace. "The girls wouldn't stop pestering me about coming to see you while we were in the city."

Dennis stood in his doorway, unsure how to react. The only other person who ever came in his apartment was his landlady, *and I couldn't keep her out even if I wanted to*, he thought. Nevertheless, the detective couldn't help but smile at the twins standing in front of him with smiles on their faces and mud caked to their soccer jerseys.

"Well don't just stand there," he said. "Come on in. Leave those cleats by the door, though. You don't need to be tracking mud all through the apartment."

The girls did as 'Uncle Dennis' said, and their mom smiled over their heads at her ex-husband. "Thank you," she silently mouthed.

He shrugged his shoulders and smiled in response.

"Okay, soccer heroes, who wants some ice cream?"

Leading the way into the kitchen, Dennis handed his ex a bottle of water and opened the freezer. *Please let there be ice cream in here. I don't even remember the last time I went grocery shopping.*

"Oooh, Uncle Dennis! Do you have a dog?"

"Huh?" Seeing the water bowl on the floor, he said, "oh, no. That's for Murphy . . . my cat."

Jennifer choked on her drink. "You, Dennis Van Hatcher, own a cat?"

"Is that so hard to imagine?"

"Well, yeah, actually. It is."

"Keeps me company. Low maintenance."

"Ah, yes, of course," she said with a mocking grin. "Uncle Dennis would never want a relationship – pet or human – that required too much from him."

Dennis knew his ex-wife was joking but glared at her all the same. "I don't have time for anything else. You should know that better than anyone."

"Where is he?" one of the girls asked, cutting into the conversation.

"Hiding. He's not used to strangers being in his apartment."

"So we can't see him?" her sister said with a frown.

"No, he's probably best left alone back there."

Jennifer laughed. "I can tell why you two get along so well. You're both grumpy old men."

****

On the other side of the East River, in a rapidly gentrifying area of the South Bronx, Detective Smith and her husband sat down to dinner.

"How's the team looking so far?" Vanessa asked in between bites of chicken and potatoes.

"Too soon to tell really," her husband replied. Roman Smith taught Algebra and Geometry at Mott Hall High School in Harlem and was the coach of the boys' basketball team. "Won't know anything until we get some more practice time in," he added. "They've been playing no-rules street ball all summer and come into the gym thinking it's MMA with a hoop at either end."

Vanessa laughed at her husband's description. "You'll whip them into shape. You always do."

"Yeah, and if they don't listen I can always threaten to sic my detective wife on them, right?"

Vanessa sighed and put her fork down on the table. "Why do you have to be like that?"

"What? You asked about my work so I asked about your work."

"No, you *accused* me about my work. Like I'm the bad

175

guy. Like I should be riding in the back of the cop car instead of the front."

"Right, right, of course. How dare anyone say anything bad about the great and magisterial New York City Police Department? Never mind the fact that my students throw shade whenever I mention your job. Never mind the fact that every time my phone rings and it's an unknown number, my heart drops to my stomach because I worry that they're calling to tell me you've been killed in the line of duty. Never mind the fact that you're never home, that I'm always second fiddle to whatever case you're working on, and that when you do happen to grace the apartment with your presence you're all bitchy and stressed out."

Vanessa stood up from the table and walked her plate over to the sink. "If I'm such a bitch while I'm here, then maybe it's better if I leave."

"Maybe so."

Detective Smith put her badge back around her neck and threw her NYPD windbreaker over her shoulders. When Roman made no effort to stop her, she walked out the front of the apartment and slammed the door behind her. As she cranked her car to drive back to the precinct, a river of tears rolled down Vanessa's cheeks.

FIFTY

The next morning, having run out of other theories, Detective Van Hatcher decided to revisit the two people who knew the victim's secrets.

His first stop was the Law Offices of Creasy, Evans, and Tumlin.

"Back again," Joe Tumlin said when the detective walked into his office.

"Back again," Dennis agreed.

"I'm afraid my answer hasn't changed. Anything Tom Wilson and I talked about is still confidential."

"What about your conversations with the rest of the family?"

"It depends," Tumlin replied. "Do you have any specific questions?"

"What was their relationship like with the victim? Was he on the outs with anyone?"

The lawyer laughed and shook his head. "Tom Wilson was never on the outs with anybody. He had a magnetic personality . . . you couldn't help but like the guy."

"So he never said anything to you about family trouble? Problems with the crew of the yacht? Problems with anybody, for that matter?"

"That's confidential."

Dennis closed his eyes and growled. "I could sit here asking you questions for the next hour and you'd just keep saying 'that's confidential', wouldn't you?"

"Yep, pretty much."

"C'mon, man. Give me something to work with here. Don't you want to see justice for your client?"

"Of course I do. And if there were anything I could tell you that might help, I would. But there isn't."

****

Forty-five minutes later, Dennis ran into the same brick wall in the office of Father Gerry. St. Monica's pastor was as warm and welcoming as always, but was equally unwilling to reveal Tom Wilson's secrets.

"The Seal of the Confessional is ironclad, Detective. There is no wiggle room."

"What about mandatory reporting laws for abuse?"

"New York law is silent on the matter," replied the priest, "but Vatican law is not. I cannot, under *any* circumstances, disclose to you or anyone else what a penitent reveals to me during confession."

Dennis sighed. "You're the second person today to clam up and claim privilege on me."

"Are you Catholic, Detective?"

"No. My mom was Presbyterian, but I've never really been a church person."

"In the Roman Catholic Church, we take confessional privilege very seriously. If I were to break that privilege, break the Seal of the Confessional, I would automatically be excommunicated from the Church."

Dennis jumped on the priest's words. "So he confessed to something?"

"I can't comment either way. What I will tell you is that the end of Mr. Wilson's life was filled with inner turmoil. His mind was not at peace, which is why I believe he sought out the Church to provide rest for his soul."

"Do you think he could have killed himself?"

Gerry thought for a minute before shaking his head.

"No. I don't think so. Tom was upset, he was troubled, but I don't think he would kill himself. He had too many people depending on him, and Tom valued loyalty and duty above all else."

****

"Any luck?" Vanessa asked when her partner returned to the precinct.

"Nada," Dennis replied. "Zilch. Squat." He let out a deep breath. "I think it's about time to close the lid on Tom Wilson."

"Really?"

Van Hatcher nodded. "We've talked to everybody. Some of them twice. We've reviewed every scrap of evidence. Run every test under the sun. We're still coming up empty."

"Don't get me wrong," Dennis added, "that is one screwed up family. They're in serious need of counseling. But all of the evidence points to an accident. Everyone else checks out."

"What about people not on the boat?" Vanessa asked, not wanting to give up yet.

"There weren't any unexplained fingerprints, and we checked the vic's blood for rare poisons, remember?"

"But what if somebody – somebody wearing gloves – came onboard under cover of darkness and killed him?"

"'Under cover of darkness'?"

"Yeah."

"Okay sure, Tom Clancy."

"No, seriously."

"Seriously," Dennis said, "the odds of a Navy SEAL-style raid on the ship are incredibly, incredibly small. Besides, they wouldn't push him overboard where he might have a chance to survive. They would've put a bullet in his head, taken him away, and fed him to the sharks."

Vanessa put her hands on her hips and cocked her head to the side. "Who's the mystery writer now?"

Her partner laughed. "Neither of us, I'm afraid. Look, the simple fact is that with our main suspects cleared, no suspicious financial activity, no mistresses in the closet or archenemies at rival companies, and the victim's own well-documented excessive drinking, the best and most logical conclusion is that it was an accident. Tom Wilson did what he shouldn't have and mixed alcohol with sleeping pills. Happens all the time. But he was unfortunate enough to fall overboard."

Smith nodded her head. "You're right. It just seems like a failure somehow, you know? For us to say it was an accident."

"It does feel incomplete, you're right," Dennis said, pulling open a desk drawer to grab a 'CLOSED' stamp. After scribbling 'accident' in the line next to cause of death, he pushed the red ink onto the file and brought an end to the Tom Wilson investigation.

Standing up from his desk, Dennis said, "it's not a failure if it's the truth."

FIFTY-ONE

Two days after the police stopped investigating his father's death, Ryan Wilson left home for the start of a new school year.

Located on the coast of Rhode Island in Middletown, St. George's School was a bastion of East Coast wealth and privilege – and thus a fitting site for Ryan's education. Founded in 1896, the school claimed the Astor and Bush families as prominent alumni and maintained its Episcopal identity, with multiple chapel services each week.

It was during one of those services, the first of the new fall semester, that the presiding reverend asked the student body to join in a special prayer "for the Wilson family as they struggle to cope with such a sudden, tragic loss."

Later, back in his dorm room, Ryan tossed himself down on his twin-sized bed and looked up at the ceiling. His six-foot frame left his feet dangling off the edge.

"Did he really have to call me out like that?"

"Who?" asked Finn, Ryan's best friend and a fellow Fourth Former – or sophomore – at St. George's.

"The Reverend. 'Let us pray especially for the Wilson family . . .'"

"I dunno," the other boy replied, sitting down in the chair by Ryan's desk. "I thought it was kinda nice of him. It's not like there's anybody here who doesn't know what happened."

"Oh, you know what happened? Can you fill me in? Maybe call the police while you're at it and tell them too. Because I don't have a fucking clue, and apparently they don't either. 'Accident' my ass."

Finn put his hands up in self-defense. "I'm sorry. I didn't mean . . . I'm sorry, alright?"

Ryan sighed and rested his head back on his pillow. "Just leave, okay?"

Finn nodded and stood up from the chair. "Sure. D'ya want the door open or closed?"

"Closed," Ryan replied. "Definitely closed."

****

MaryJo and the faculty and staff at St. George's had hoped that the beginning of the school year would distract Ryan from everything that happened over the summer. A new location, a new focus, even a new Varsity tennis team.

But Ryan's grades slipped from the outset, he locked himself in his room as often as possible, and three weeks into the semester he announced that he was quitting the tennis team.

"But dude, why?" asked Finn.

Ryan shrugged his shoulders. "I only ever played because I wanted to impress my dad. It was something he and I could do together that nobody else in the family did. Now that he's gone . . . what's the point?"

After hearing the news, the tennis coach called Mrs. Wilson, who promptly called her husband's former tennis partner: Derrick Clark.

"Will you talk to him?" she pleaded. "I can't seem to get through to him these days, and I know he'll regret it if he quits the team. Maybe he'll listen to you."

The police commissioner called Ryan on his way home from work that night.

"I know why you're calling and it's not going to work," the boy said when he answered the phone. "I'm quitting."

"Okay," Derrick replied. "Doesn't matter to me either way."

"It doesn't?"

"It's your life. If you don't want to play tennis, then don't play. But not playing because you're upset that your dad won't be around to see it is stupid."

"I'm not stupid!"

"I didn't say you were. I said that would be a stupid reason to quit. If you're gonna quit, at least do it for a valid reason. A reason you won't regret later."

"Like what?" Ryan asked.

"Well, maybe think of it the opposite way, hmm? Your dad loved tennis, and he loved that you played. He would beam with pride when he talked about how great it would be if you followed in his footsteps and suited up for Harvard too."

"He did?"

"Oh yeah," Derrick said, smiling and nodding his head. "The last time we played, he told me that you were going to be good enough to beat him soon. Tom never would've admitted it to you," he added, "but the idea thrilled him. I think you're the only person in the world who he wouldn't have minded losing to."

"Dad hated losing."

"He did. But as much as he hated losing, he loved you more."

Silence fell over the phone and the commissioner could hear what sounded like muffled crying on the other end of the line.

"So you see, Ryan, you have to keep playing. You have to prove your dad right. He said you could be the best Wilson yet, and he meant it."

The teenager paused to wipe his eyes. "Okay. I'll play. Do you think . . . no, nevermind."

"What?"

"Do you think we could play a match when I'm home over break? If you have time?"

Derrick smiled and he felt tears welling in his own eyes. "Absolutely. I'd love to."

FIFTY-TWO

In late September, after avoiding it for as long as possible, MaryJo asked the butler to drive her to Wilson|Cole so she could clean out her husband's office.

"It's good to see you, Mrs. Wilson," said the receptionist. "Oh, and you too, big guy. What's your name?"

"This is Gus. I hope it's okay that I brought him with me."

"Of course. No problem at all. And ma'am, let me say how sorry I am for your loss."

"Thank you," MaryJo replied, still unsure how to respond when people said that to her. *Thank you for being sorry? That sounds like I'm happy they're sad*, she thought. *Although I guess that's partly true. If they're sad, too, then I don't have to be sad alone.*

"Is his office unlocked?" she asked.

"No ma'am. Let me get the key and I'll take you down there."

Left alone in Tom's old office, MaryJo walked around the room and took it all in. *This is the first time I've been in here by myself*, she thought. *Probably because Thomas never left it.* The nature of the New York investment world – combined with his workaholic personality – meant that MaryJo's husband spent more time at the office than he ever did at home.

This is where he really lived.

Even though he was a banker, Thomas decorated his office with bookcases full of economic treatises and other large volume dissertations. His desk, on the other hand, was covered in family photos. Spanning thirty-eight years, they began with a Memorial Day party when he and MaryJo were first dating and ran all the way up to the celebration of his granddaughter Harper's first birthday.

Mrs. Wilson picked up the most recent picture and

184

smiled. Everyone was wearing party hats, and both Madison and Harper were covered head to toe in birthday cake.

"That was a great day, wasn't it, Gus?"

The dog sniffed the frame but lost interest when he discovered it wasn't food.

MaryJo placed the photo back on her husband's desk before picking it up again. *Might as well start here.* She wrapped the picture frame in a piece of newspaper that she had brought with her and then proceeded to cover and pack the other photos on Thomas' desk.

Gus, undisturbed by the meaning of the moment, padded across the room and curled up in a corner.

"I see you're going to be a big help today," MaryJo told the dog. Placing the last picture in a box, she turned her attention to the filing cabinets lining the far wall.

Outside the office, Charles Cole stopped at the receptionist's desk. "Did I see MaryJo Wilson walk by earlier?"

"Yes sir. She came to clear out Tom's personal effects."

Charles nodded and looked down the hall toward his business partner's corner office. Walking to the open doorway, he knocked and waited.

MaryJo looked up from her seat on the floor.

"Oh, Charles, hi. Don't worry about the mess," she said, gesturing to the files strewn around her. "I'll have it all straightened up before I leave."

"No bother," he replied, stepping fully into the office and closing the door behind him. "We've already removed the active client files. Everything that's left is either personal stuff or things from years ago. Decades ago some of it."

"I know. The time flew by."

Charles pulled a chair closer to where MaryJo was working. "How is everybody?" he asked. "How are you? You know, since it happened?

"I feel bad that I haven't stopped by more to check in," Cole continued, "but we've been slammed here trying to shuffle clients and fill gaps. It's amazing how much Tom still handled himself."

MaryJo shook her head and resumed sifting through the papers in front of her. "No need to apologize. I understand. And we're . . . well, we're getting by. Tripp is burying himself in his work, or at least that's what Anya tells me. You probably have a better idea of what he's been up to than I do," she added, referencing her son's role as a junior partner at Wilson|Cole. "Kay is busy trying to devise some sort of foundation or memorial or something in Thomas' memory. Who knows what it will end up being. I think working on it is helping her cope, though."

"And Ryan?"

MaryJo looked down at the floor to mask the flash of guilt that ran across her face. The same guilt she felt every time her youngest son came up in a conversation with Charles. Glancing back up, she replied, "he's doing okay, I think. He's back up at school now, which the counselor said is good for him. Keeps him busy."

Does he know? MaryJo wondered, scanning Charles' eyes for any signs of recognition. *Does he care?*

Much to MaryJo's relief, the face of her late husband's business partner remained measured and appropriately but not excessively concerned.

"How about you?" he asked.

MaryJo breathed a sigh of relief. Ever since Tom's death, she had been avoiding Charles out of fear that he would seize the moment to confront her about Ryan.

"I'm fine," she answered with a forced smile.

"MaryJo . . ."

"No, honestly, I'm okay. The police investigation is over. It didn't give us any real answers, but at least they aren't poking around our lives anymore. In the meantime, I'm taking it day by day. I'm counting my blessings and focusing on what I still have rather than what I lost."

Charles lowered himself from his chair to the floor and

took MaryJo's hands in his, forcing her to stop sorting papers.

"That's a fantastic answer and I bet it goes over really well at lunch with the ladies. But . . . look at me, MJ," he said, using the nickname only he had ever called her. "Look at me," Charles repeated.

When she finally glanced up through tear-filled eyes, he said: "I've known you for thirty-eight years. I knew you very well at one point, if you recall."

"I'd rather not."

"Nevertheless, we go way back. And I'm not buying that 'I'm fine' answer of yours."

MaryJo sighed and used her sleeve to wipe a tear off her cheek.

"Here," Charles said, reaching into his jacket pocket and passing her his handkerchief.

"Thanks." MaryJo dabbed both eyes that had suddenly filled with tears. "You're right," the widow admitted. "I'm not okay. I'm not okay at all."

Hearing MaryJo begin to cry, Gus left his post in the corner and walked across the office to lie down beside his owner. The big chocolate lab rested his head on her thigh and sighed.

Despite her tears, MaryJo smiled. "This big fella keeps me going. He's always been a sweet dog, but I swear he's like a certified therapist now. I don't know how I'd get through the day without him."

Charles rubbed the dog's head in appreciation. "What a good boy."

After a second, he added, "if you ever need anything, MJ, anything at all, please call me. Anytime, day or night. I'm here for you." He paused and lowered his voice. "I'm always here for you."

MaryJo nodded her head and blew her nose into the handkerchief. "I know." Looking up at Charles, she said: "you should get back to work, though. So should I. It's going to take forever to sort through these files."

"Right," Charles replied, knowing that was his cue. He used the chair to push himself up off the floor. "*Oof.* That was a lot easier twenty years ago. I'm right down the hall if you need anything, MJ."

"Thanks Charlie," MaryJo said, finally returning the nickname gesture.

When he reached the door, Cole turned to look back at MaryJo, who had already resumed sorting through her late husband's files.

Now wasn't the time, he told himself. *Later. When she's stronger.*

Charles had intended to ask MaryJo about Ryan that day – to lay to rest once and for all his creeping suspicion that the youngest Wilson was actually a Cole. *My height, my build. Hell, he even has my nose*, he thought. Even though Ryan's reported father, Tom, was also tall and athletic, Charles always wondered. Especially since the boy was born at the tail end of his torrid, secret affair with MaryJo.

Now's not the time, though, he thought again. *I'll do it when she's stronger.*

FIFTY-THREE

Several weeks later, on a crisp day in early November, Kay and Tripp met for lunch at Michael's on West 55th. It was a little too trendy and celebrity for Tripp's tastes, but Kay loved it for those very same reasons.

"You never know who you'll bump into here. This city is all about connections."

Her brother rolled his eyes. "Yes. I know. I grew up here too, remember? And isn't this place a little high end for you?" Tripp asked. "With your and Luke's finances?"

Kay shrugged. "Not after this afternoon, it won't be."

"Already spending your inheritance before you even know what you'll get?"

"Don't give me that," Kay snapped. "You know as well as I do that we're going to wake up tomorrow anywhere from $10 million to $15 million richer. Pretending otherwise makes you look common."

The ultimate insult in her world, Tripp thought. *Sometimes I'm amazed we're related.*

"So," Kay said after they ordered their drinks, "how's Anya?"

"Doing well. She has her six month check-up next week."

"Still keeping the baby's gender a secret?"

Tripp nodded. "Even to us. I think it'll be more fun that way. There are so few genuine surprises in life."

"Babies are full of them, I can promise you that," Kay replied. Switching topics, she asked: "have you seen Mom lately?"

"Not in a couple weeks. I've been slammed at work. You?"

"We met for brunch on Saturday. I try to pick activities where we have to go somewhere to make sure she's getting out of the house. Otherwise she'd sit around in her robe,

189

drink wine, and watch cable news all the time."

"You're probably right," Tripp said. "Every time I talk to her she rattles on and on about the dog. I think she's channeling all of her grief about Dad into taking care of Gus. That's weird, right?"

Kay shook her head. "I don't think so. I think it's good for her. I've seen other women who lost their husbands turn to alcohol or prescription drugs or even outrageous shopping binges to try to deal with their pain. Letting her dog sleep in the bed with her and wanting to take him everywhere she goes seems like a perfectly fine, non-destructive way to cope."

"Yeah. I guess you're right."

"Regardless, we'll get a much better idea of how she's doing this afternoon at the reading of the will."

FIFTY-FOUR

At 3pm sharp, six members of the Wilson family arrived at the lawyer's office. It was a short walk for Tripp – only two blocks away from his desk at Wilson|Cole.

"I still don't understand why we had to wait ninety days to do this," Luke said while the family waited in the reception area.

"Because that's what it said in the will," replied Tripp.

"Yeah, but it's not like waiting changes anything," Luke pressed.

Ryan had taken the day off from school to be there, and he turned and glared at his brother-in-law. "Would you drop it already? Geez. You're only here because you hope you can take Kay's money and pay off your gambling debts."

"Come on, everyone," said MaryJo. "Let's keep this civil, please." The death of her husband had hit her hard, and Mrs. Wilson looked like she had aged ten years in the past three months.

Noticing their mom's pale skin and extreme weight loss, and hearing the exhaustion in her voice, MaryJo's children and their spouses all nodded their heads and agreed to behave.

A few minutes later, a large mahogany door swung open and Joe Tumlin, the family lawyer, stood on the other side. "Great, you're all here. Come on in."

"I'm going to start with a brief financial overview," Mr. Tumlin said after everyone joined him in his office. "That way, when I start talking division of assets, you'll have a better idea of what's in play."

Hearing no objections, Tumlin opened the folder in front of him and started reading aloud.

"The two residences, Manhattan and the Hamptons, are worth $24 million. Eighteen for the townhouse and six for the summer home, with outstanding mortgages totaling $9 million. Both were well on their way to being paid off. Mr. Wilson had approximately $75 million in stocks, bonds, and other investments," the lawyer continued, "and $30 million in savings, CDs, and other checking account balances.

"Another twelve in boat and car assets, fifteen in retirement plans, and of course the $20 million life insurance policy." The advisor looked down at his sheet of paper. "Oh, yes, there's also $34 million in other, miscellaneous assets."

"Like what?" asked MaryJo.

"Paintings, vintage wines, a rather valuable collection of rare books on loan to his alma mater."

"Right. Of course. Sorry."

"No need to apologize, Mrs. Wilson. Shall I continue?"

MaryJo nodded.

"Your husband lived relatively debt-free, with the exception of the residential mortgages. Total debts equaled only $9.5 million. The funeral and estate processing fees will add up to about 200 grand. And Mr. Wilson gave $10 million from his estate in upon-death charitable contributions."

"To whom?" asked Kay.

"Umm," Tumlin said, flipping through a stack of papers, "Mount Sinai Children's Hospital, the NYC Police Foundation, and . . ."

He paused.

"And where?"

"Ironically enough, the Bahamas Air Sea Rescue Association."

MaryJo gasped and dissolved in a flood of tears. Kay put her arms around her mom's frail shoulders. "Shhh, it's okay. It's okay."

"No it's not, dammit! Stop saying that. It's not okay!"

Tom Wilson's longtime private counsel squirmed in his chair, uncomfortable at being caught in the middle of MaryJo's outburst.

"We can . . . we can continue this some other time, Mrs. Wilson."

192

"No," she replied, shaking her head. The widow sniffed back tears and wiped her eyes. "We're here now. Let's finish this."

"Okay. Where was I? Oh, right. Taxes. New York's estate tax is sixteen percent on all assets over $2 million, so that's approximately thirty-three and a quarter – leaving a net taxable estate of just under $157 million. Federal estate tax will be another sixty and half, which means when it's all said and done you'll have about $96 million."

The lawyer paused. "Are there any questions so far?"

When no one replied, he took a deep breath and looked back down at the paper in front of him. "Okay, now to the division of remaining assets."

Chairs squeaked around the room as the deceased's heirs leaned forward, eager to learn the extent of their newfound wealth.

Vultures, the lawyer thought.

"Half of the remaining estate is to be left to Mrs. Wilson," he said, nodding in the direction of MaryJo. "Each of the natural-born children – Thomas III, Katherine, and Ryan – are to receive fifteen percent, with Ryan's share held in trust until he reaches the age of twenty-five."

Sitting silently in her chair, MaryJo breathed a sigh of relief. *He never found out about Ryan. Thank God.*

"That's only 95%," Tripp said, doing the math in his head.

"Yes, that's correct. The remaining five percent was left to Tripp and Anya's firstborn child, to be held in trust until he or she is twenty-five years old."

Kay's jaw dropped and she squinted her eyes together in confusion. "Hold on. His firstborn kid gets five percent but my already living daughters don't get anything?"

"That's correct."

"What kind of bullshit is that?" asked Luke.

Joe Tumlin held his hands out to gesture that he didn't understand either. "I didn't make the decision," the attorney said in self-defense. "I simply drafted the bequests according to Mr. Wilson's instructions."

"Mom, come on," said Kay. "This has got to be some kind of mistake."

MaryJo sat motionless in her chair, trying to process the unexpected inclusion in her husband's estate. "I don't know, honey. Your father never told me anything about changing his will."

"Why don't we just divide it in three?" asked Tripp. "Take the five percent and split it? I mean, I know it's my kid getting the money but I still I don't think he or she should have it over Dad's other grandkids."

"Unfortunately, that's not your decision to make," said Tom's lawyer. "My job as executor is to follow Mr. Wilson's wishes. Once the accounts are settled, the five percent will be placed directly in a trust for Tripp and Anya's baby."

"We'll challenge it in court," Luke declared. "Five percent is nearly $5 million. Maddie and Harper deserve their fair share."

Mr. Tumlin shook his head. "I understand that you're all upset and confused, but this isn't a challengeable issue. Mr. Wilson made his decision of sound mind and body and with a logically coherent reason for doing so."

"Which was?" MaryJo asked, her voice barely above a whisper.

"I'm sorry, ma'am, but I can't tell you that."

Luke scoffed. "Surely all that attorney-client bullshit ends when the client dies."

"Actually, in the state of New York, it doesn't."

Luke stood up from his chair. "C'mon Kay. This guy is clearly biased. We'll get our own lawyer to contest the will. Everyone in this room knows that Tom was drunk off his ass for the last several months of his life. This won't stand," Luke said, walking out the door. "This won't stand."

194

FIFTY-FIVE

Later that night, after spending several hours trying to calm down Kay and Luke and assuring them that she would make things right with the inheritances in her own will, MaryJo kicked off her stiletto heels and poured herself a tall glass of Screaming Eagle cabernet.

Picking up the phone, she dialed a number she knew by heart.

"Derrick, it's MaryJo. Can you talk for a minute?"

"Absolutely," Commissioner Clark replied. "Just give me one second."

At his apartment on the other side of Central Park, Derrick passed the television remote to his wife and signaled to her to keep watching the show rather than pausing it.

"Who is it?" Cindy asked.

Clark covered the phone with his hand. "MaryJo Wilson," he whispered before turning and walking from the living room to his study. Closing the door behind him, New York's top cop propped one hip up on the edge of his desk.

"What can I do for you, MaryJo?"

A loud sigh echoed on the other end of the line.

"Thomas' will was read today," she began, and Derrick heard a mixture of sadness and confusion in her voice. "It all looked like we expected . . . except for one thing."

"What's that?"

"Tripp's baby. Well, the baby Anya is carrying now."

"What about it?" Derrick asked, standing up and walking around to his chair. *I have a feeling I'm going to want to be seated for this.* Tom Wilson was his best friend, a pillar of success and bastion of family values, but the same instinct that made Clark a great police officer was also telling him that the other shoe was about to drop in the investigation.

"Thomas singled out that baby for an extra share of inheritance," said MaryJo, "and nobody knows why. I mean, like I said, there were no surprises up to that point. Surviving spouse: that's me. Three children: Tripp, Kay, and Ryan. He didn't mention Madison or Harper or any other future grandchildren . . ."

"But he singled out Tripp's first born?"

"Exactly," Mrs. Wilson replied, and the commissioner could picture her perfectly-coifed hair bobbing back and forth as she spoke. "I don't get it, Derrick. It doesn't make any sense."

"What did the lawyer say?"

"That he can't tell us anything because of confidentiality rules."

"But Tom is dead."

"That's what we said," MaryJo responded, the sadness returning to her voice. "He told us that it doesn't matter. He still can't say."

The police commissioner sank back in his leather chair. "I agree that it's . . . odd. To say the least."

"Thomas never said anything to you about changing his will?"

"No. Nothing. We never talked about that kind of stuff."

MaryJo breathed heavily into the phone. "I didn't think you would have. He never really talked about it with me either. But now with all of this happening . . . I don't know, Derrick. I feel like there was this whole other Thomas that I didn't know. Secret meetings with a priest. Changing his will to give money to other people." Her sigh dissolved into sobs. "I don't know who I can trust anymore. I don't even feel safe in my own house."

"If you feel that uncomfortable at home, take Gus and check into The Carlyle for a couple of nights." Derrick paused. "What, umm . . . was there anything you wanted from me or were you just calling to tell me about it?"

"What I want to know is if this changes anything," MaryJo replied. "I know your detectives concluded that it was an accident, but does this make things different?"

"Not for the investigation, no. If somebody confessed or a boater came forward and said he was in those same waters that night – then we might have something. But an unexpected bequest in a will? No."

If it said 'I leave half my estate to my illegitimate kids and mistress', he thought, *that'd also be a different story.* Clark didn't share his thoughts with Tom's widow. *Don't want to upset her even more.*

MaryJo sighed again and Derrick could almost hear her nodding her head in resignation.

"Okay," she said. "I figured I should at least ask."

"Of course. You can call anytime. Oh hey, MaryJo?"

"Yes?"

"I almost forgot. I'm playing tennis with Ryan on Saturday before he goes back to school. He told you that, right?"

"No, but that's great. He'll enjoy that."

"Well, Cindy and I thought we might have you two over for dinner afterward if you want."

MaryJo smiled. "That sounds wonderful. I could do with a night out of the house."

"Excellent. I'll tell Cindy to call you tomorrow and work out the details."

"Perfect. Thanks for taking my call and listening to my rambling, Derrick. I know you're very busy and I really appreciate it."

"Anytime, MaryJo. Anytime."

After hanging up the phone, Derrick stood up from his chair and stretched his arms over his head. *What a mess,* he thought. *You couldn't just leave things as they should be, could you Tommy?*

"But why Tripp's kid?" Clark asked, still talking to his deceased friend. "If anything, the only surprise I expected was something about Ryan."

Derrick's thoughts flashed back sixteen years to an autumn afternoon on the tennis courts.

~~~

It was Tom's turn to serve. As he bounced the ball in front of him several times and tossed it high in the air, he said: "I don't think this kid is mine."

The serve whizzed past Derrick for an ace.

"W-what?" he asked, walking toward the net.

Tom shrugged his shoulders, pulled another yellow tennis ball out of his pocket, and began bouncing it in preparation for his next hit. "Are we going to play or what?"

"Not until you tell me what's going on. Why would you think that? You and MaryJo are wonderful together."

Taking a few steps toward the net, Tom cocked his head to the side. "Eh, things haven't been great lately. I work all the time. She complains about it all the time. And now that the kids are grown, she's home alone a lot."

'Alone' with a housekeeper and a butler, Derrick thought, but didn't say anything.

"I don't know," Tom said, shrugging his shoulders. "There's been something different about her lately. Then this surprise pregnancy . . ."

"Are you going to say anything?"

"No. I have no proof. I can't throw my marriage and family into chaos with that kind of accusation on the basis of a hunch."

"I know of quite a few business deals that you went with on a hunch."

"True," Tom replied, balancing the tennis ball on his racket and refusing to look his friend in the eye. "But that was business. This is family."

~~~

Commissioner Clark thought back to that conversation as he stood in his study, contemplating his next move. Part of him said he should leave things as they were. *What you told MaryJo on the phone wasn't untrue*, he reminded himself. "Then again," he said aloud, "Tom Wilson had a reason for everything he did. He wouldn't leave this loose end for his family without what he thought was a very, very good reason."

FIFTY-SIX

The next morning, Dennis Van Hatcher's desk phone rang.

"Hello?"

"Van Hatcher? It's Commissioner Clark."

Oh shit, the detective thought. *What now?*

Dennis knew it was an honor for the commissioner to think so well of him and assign him so many high-profile cases, *but sometimes it'd be nice if he'd leave me alone for a little while.*

"Good morning, Commissioner," Dennis said, masking his annoyance. "What can I do for you, sir?"

"What are you working on right now?"

"Whatever you tell me to, sir."

"No, seriously," said Derrick. "What kind of cases do you and your partner have going?"

"I'm on an armed robbery/assault and Detective Smith has a carjacking."

"I'd like you to do a little digging for me on something," the commissioner said. "Unofficially."

Van Hatcher grabbed a pen and a pad of paper to write down notes. "What is it?"

"The Wilson case again. Tom's will was finally read yesterday."

"What took so long?" Dennis asked.

"There was a clause in the will saying they had to wait ninety days after he died. I have no idea why. But anyway, everything was pretty standard except for one item. Tom left an extra inheritance for Tripp and Anya's baby."

"Anya . . . she's the one who's pregnant now, right?"

"Yep."

"The other grandkids didn't get anything?"

"Nope."

Sitting at his desk, Dennis scribbled notes on the paper.

"Okay. We'll see what we can find."

"Thanks, Van Hatcher. I appreciate it."

After hanging up the phone, the detective walked to a wall of filing cabinets on the other end of the floor and pulled open the drawer marked 'W'.

"Wilson," he said, lifting out a large manila folder. "Here it is."

Dennis opened the information in front of him and read while he walked back to his desk. "Okay Tommy . . . what aren't you telling us? What are you hiding?" Dennis added, repeating the question he had often asked during the official investigation.

The veteran detective looked down at a list of everyone who was on *The Arvid* when Tom Wilson went missing.

"It's not the crew," he concluded. "If one of them tried to sneak out, the others would've heard him. And they couldn't have all been in on it together, because the captain wouldn't stand for it. No motive. No animosity." Dennis shook his head. "They all lost something by virtue of their boss dying. So they're out.

"The youngest son seems clean. He idolized his father and, based on what the commissioner told me, his life went into a tailspin after the vic died." Van Hatcher sat back down in his chair. "So it's not the kid.

"The son-in-law was gambling online the entire time and the daughter was asleep with the two granddaughters," Dennis recalled from his notes. "The gambling video confirmed it. Kay and the two little girls can be seen in the background of the footage the whole time."

He let out a frustrated sigh. "The older son, Tripp, also doesn't fit the profile. Happy, successful, expecting his first baby. Plus he lost his biggest ally at the office when his dad died. And I don't see the daughter-in-law doing much of anything except shopping. Although, it is their kid who stands to inherit the extra money." He paused. "Except nobody knew that until yesterday.

201

"Which leaves Mrs. Wilson," Dennis concluded. "The instigator behind this entire investigation." He pulled a picture of the widow out of the case folder and held it up in front of him. "You wouldn't put me through all of this shit just to cover up the fact that you killed him, would you?"

"Whatcha got?" asked Vanessa as she walked to her desk, her purse slung over one shoulder and a coffee in each hand. Passing one of the cups to her partner, Detective Smith sat down across from Dennis.

"The Wilson file," he replied, putting MaryJo's picture back in the folder and taking the lid off the coffee cup to help it cool faster. "Thanks for this," Dennis added.

"No problem. Why do you have out the Wilson file?"

"The commissioner called me a few minutes ago. Said something fishy happened at the reading of Tom's will and now the ruling of an accidental death isn't sitting right with him."

"Are we reopening the case?" Vanessa asked.

"Not officially. Clark wants us to dig around a little more, though, in light of the new information."

"Which is?"

"Apparently our friend Tom left most of his estate to his wife, followed by equal portions to his three kids."

"Yeah," Vanessa said sarcastically, "that sounds really fishy to me."

"Wait for it. The unborn grandkid also got a share."

"Which unborn grandkid? Tripp and Anya's baby?"

"Yep."

****

Later that afternoon, Dennis and Vanessa relocated from their precinct office to McSorley's pub.

"My brain thinks better when it's oiled up on french fry grease," Dennis said with a smile.

"I bet your heart doesn't beat better, though."

202

"If I wanted someone to nag me about my health, I'd get married again," Van Hatcher replied. Despite the added stress of the Wilson case, the veteran detective was in a good mood. He'd had a great date the night before with a pretty rookie from the 12th Precinct.

"Speaking of marriages," he said, "you're married. Have you ever seen your father-in-law's hip? Like the part that would normally be covered by clothes?"

"What? No. I don't particularly want to either. Why?"

"It's something Anya Wilson said to me in passing at the funeral. I didn't think anything of it at the time, but . . ."

"What'd she say?" Vanessa asked.

"There were a couple of members of the vic's fraternity, or 'final club' I think they called it, at his funeral. I talked to her for a few minutes and mentioned how it was nice of his college buddies to show up. She said something about how they were all really close, including having to get the club's symbol tattooed on their hip as a rite of initiation.

"I don't know," Dennis said while they waited on their food order to arrive. "I agree with the commissioner . . . there's something fishy going on. Dude changes his will at the last minute to leave extra money to a random grandkid and the lawyer won't say why. I looked up the statute. 'Privilege' usually goes away on a will when somebody dies, but it stays for information that would 'disgrace the memory of the deceased'. Plus, in addition to changing his will, Tom started going to church every week. The priest said that Wilson had a lot of 'inner turmoil'. Add to that his daughter-in-law knowing random private stuff about him . . ."

"You know the obvious answer," Vanessa replied.

"What?"

"The grandkid is really his kid."

Dennis scrunched up his face. "Ah, gross."

"Why else would he change his will to benefit an unborn grandchild to the detriment of his living granddaughters? Maybe if it would be the first grandkid. Or if they knew it was a boy so it's his first grandson and heir or whatever. But without any of that?" Vanessa raised her eyebrows in suspicion. "I think we should have a little chat with the mom of New York's richest fetus."

FIFTY-SEVEN

Purchase, NY's main shopping mall, The Westchester, was a three-level, 133-store ode to upper class fashion. Anchored by Nordstrom and Neiman Marcus, The Westchester was also home to a small boutique called 'Dubois' – Anya Wilson's store. Although it was surrounded by higher-end brands like Kate Spade and Burberry, Dubois carried a more relaxed clothing line and had lower prices to match. Its affordability and 'wear-ability' made the younger Mrs. Wilson an instant success.

Walking into the store, Detective Smith could see that the financial reports weren't lying: Anya's boutique was doing quite well for itself, especially as Christmas shopping season was kicking into gear.

Thinking it would be better to confront her murder suspect woman-to-woman, particularly given the sensitive nature of their crime theory, Dennis stayed behind at the precinct. Unbeknownst to Anya, though, two uniformed officers had accompanied Vanessa and were stationed strategically outside the front and rear exits of the store.

"Detective," Anya said as she walked over. "I wasn't expecting you. Is there something I can help you with?"

"Yes, actually," Vanessa lied. "A friend of mine is getting married and I wanted to go a different route with her bridal shower gift. She and her fiancé already have all of the household things they might need, so I thought I'd get her an outfit to wear on the honeymoon."

"What a great idea. We won't have our new spring lines in for a couple of months, but I'm sure we can find something that will work." Anya led her customer over to the corner of the store. "Most of our last-season items are here. How about this?" she asked, lifting a red sundress off the rack.

"It's pretty, for sure, but I don't think she'd want a

strapless dress. She has a tattoo on her shoulder that she doesn't really like," Vanessa said, continuing to set her trap. "Until she can save enough money to get it removed, she doesn't like to wear clothes where people can see it."

Anya nodded. "I understand. That's why I never got a tattoo. I'm afraid of how it would look when I get older and saggy."

The detective couldn't help but laugh. "Good point. Yeah, my friend's is kind of like the tattoo that your father-in-law had from his fraternity. The one on his hip? It's small and usually covered up, but she still doesn't like it to show."

Vanessa paused. "Although, I guess having it on your hip would be one of the best places to hide it. That way it could only be seen when you're changing clothes or something like that."

Anya nodded and started folding a stack of sweaters in front of her.

Vanessa took a deep breath. Reaching this point with a suspect, knowing the trap was set and she was about to snap it shut, always made her nervous.

"Is that when you saw Tom's tattoo? When he was changing clothes?"

Anya's face went pale, and Detective Smith saw the other woman's hands start to tremble as she tried to continue straightening the clothing display.

"What . . . w-what do you mean?"

"The tattoo on your father-in-law's hip," Vanessa replied. "You mentioned it to my partner at the funeral." She walked around the table to stand beside Anya and leaned over, her voice dropping to a whisper. "Thing is, the only other person who knew about that tattoo was your mother-in-law. Not his friends, not his sister, not his business partner. Not even his son – your husband."

Anya placed a freshly-folded shirt on top of the stack, using her hands to brace herself on the table. Her eyes welled with tears but she stared straight ahead.

"It happened once," she said, the beginning of a slow, long-overdue expulsion of guilt from her heart.

Vanessa stood still, listening.

"Tripp was out of town. Two weeks in Hong Kong for work. I was having some car trouble, and Tom offered to help. Mechanics always think they can swindle a woman who comes into their shop." She paused to wipe a tear from her cheek. "Either that or I'm just really bad at managing staff and telling people what to do. I didn't grow up with all of this, you know," she said, cutting her eyes over at the police detective in a plea for understanding.

"It's not easy running a household that size or trying to explain your car trouble to some random guy, and Tom offered to help. My husband wasn't going to be home for another week and a half, and I didn't want the car to be completely broken down when he got back so I . . . I thought what's the harm, right? Fathers-in-law help their daughters-in-law with stuff all the time."

"Excuse me," said a customer, breaking into the conversation. "Sorry, but can I get a dressing room?"

Anya looked startled as she removed her hands from the display table. "Sure, right this way."

Detective Smith watched her murder suspect walk toward the other side of the store, knowing that a uniformed officer was waiting outside in case the woman tried to make a break for it.

Seconds later, Anya returned.

She's not running, Vanessa thought. *I bet she won't fight the charges, either.*

"Mrs. Wilson, before you keep going with your story, I need to tell you that you're under arrest. I won't handcuff you in your store or make a scene as long as you cooperate. Ok?"

Anya looked at the floor and nodded her head.

Keeping her voice low, Vanessa continued: "you have the right to remain silent. Anything you say from this point on can be used against you in court. You have the right to an attorney –"

"If I can't afford a lawyer, one will be appointed for me. I know. I watch <u>Law and Order</u>."

A small smile curved up in the corner of the detective's mouth. "Ok then."

Anya took a deep breath and exhaled. Vanessa could tell that the other woman wanted someone to talk to, someone to understand, regardless of the consequences.

Unfortunately for the younger Mrs. Wilson, that someone was a police detective.

"MaryJo was at a charity benefit that night," Anya said, picking up where she left off with the story. "We ordered Indian food for dinner." She shrugged her shoulders. "What's the harm in that, right? We were family. Better than eating alone. I drank wine and he drank scotch . . . too much. The food was spicy and we both drank too much."

Anya closed her eyes, her mind drifting back six months earlier to that fateful night in early May.

~~~

Ding dong

The doorbell echoed through Tripp and Anya's Westchester County home. Although it could get lonely at times, especially if her husband had to travel or work late, Anya didn't mind living a quiet suburban life. She knew that kind of upbringing would be better for their kids. *If we ever have kids*, she thought as she walked toward the front door. Anya and Tripp both wanted a house full of children, but after five years of marriage she still hadn't been able to get pregnant.

Anya cleared those thoughts from her mind when she saw her father-in-law standing on the front porch.

"Tom," she said with a smile as she opened the door.

"This is a surprise. Come on in."

Still in his work suit, Tom had undone the top button of his shirt and loosened his tie but otherwise looked like he was ready to conquer any boardroom on Wall Street. *Or grace the cover of GQ*, Anya thought.

"Thanks," he replied, stepping inside the foyer. "My meetings in Boston ended ahead of schedule so I caught an earlier flight, but I completely forgot that MaryJo has her charity thing tonight. Then I remembered her telling me on the phone earlier that you were having car trouble, so I figured I'd drive out and see if I can help."

"Fix my car?"

"Sure," Tom replied, holding up what Anya now recognized was a bag of tools. "I'm not just a car collector," he said. "I'm also a bit of a mechanic. Rebuilt an entire engine in high school."

"Wow. I didn't know that."

Tom nodded. "Yep. So, waddaya say? Want me to take a look?"

"Sure, absolutely. That'd be fantastic."

Anya stepped to the side and let her father-in-law lead the way to the garage. While Tom and MaryJo didn't visit often, they came by enough to know their way around the house.

As well they should, since they bought it for us, Anya thought. *A $2 million house as a wedding present*. She still couldn't believe it.

Tom set his tools down on a countertop in the garage and popped the hood of Anya's black Range Rover.

"Is there anything I can do to help?" she asked.

"Don't think so," he replied, shaking his head. "MaryJo said it's having trouble turning over? Won't start sometimes?"

Anya nodded. "Mmm hmm. That's right."

"Okay. Let me tinker with it for a little while. I'll come get you if I need anything."

Twenty minutes later, Anya returned to the garage carrying a cup of water, a glass of whisky, and a takeout menu.

"I didn't know which drink you'd prefer," she said, "and I was going to order some dinner if you want to join me."

Tom wiped his hands on the grease towel he kept stashed in his tool bag and reached for the drinks, sipping from the water before placing the glasses on the counter. "Both are appreciated. Thank you. And dinner sounds great. I haven't eaten since breakfast."

Anya smiled and held out the menu.

"Indian. Perfect. Hmm . . . I'll do the chicken vindaloo. With some cheese naan, if they have it."

"Hot, medium, or mild for the curry?"

"Hot. I love spicy food." Tom grinned. "MaryJo says I must be part-Indian because I can eat all kinds of spicy foods and it never bothers me."

Anya returned the smile. "Hot it is then. I'll let you know when it gets here."

One chicken vindaloo, one chicken tikka masala, and two cheese naans later, Tom and Anya found themselves seated on the living room sofa and using the coffee table to hold their food.

The takeout was accompanied by two bottles of alcohol: scotch for Thomas and wine for Anya.

Mr. Wilson settled back into the couch cushions and twirled his glass in his hand.

"This is a great house," he said, looking around the room.

"It is. Thank you."

Tom smiled and nodded his head, the effects of the alcohol beginning to show. "Stop thanking me. You and Tripp deserved a proper house. Nothing more."

Anya shook her head back and forth, feeling tipsy herself. "There are proper houses and then there are houses like this one."

"Not proper?"

She laughed. "Beyond proper. Amazing."

"Ahh, well, cheers to that," Tom said, clinking his glass against hers. "And cheers to you – a fantastic daughter-in-law."

Anya smiled. "I think you might be a little drunk."

"Nah, not drunk. Although that damn Indian food proved MaryJo wrong. Holy hell that was spicy."

"Mine was too," Anya commented, still tasting the curry on her lips.

"Then drink up, honey," Tom said, motioning toward the bottle of wine. "You've gotta catch up to me."

FIFTY-EIGHT

Standing in the middle of the store, Anya lowered her voice even further and looked up from the floor to glance at her confessor. Tears threatened to overrun her eyes.

"He was a really handsome man. I always thought so. I always liked the idea that Tripp would look like him some day."

"You slept together," Vanessa concluded.

Anya closed her eyes and the motion caused the tears to overflow, sending rivers streaming down her cheeks.

"Once. Only once." She sniffed and wiped the tears from her face, but it was only a temporary reprieve from the flood. "We swore we would never tell anyone. It was all going to be fine. Tripp and MaryJo would never know."

"You're carrying his baby," the detective added.

Anya placed her hands over her growing stomach and nodded her head up and down.

"You wanted to come clean. He threatened to kill you, so you had to kill him."

"What? No!"

"He wanted to come clean – guilty conscience and all of that. So you killed him to keep it all secret."

"I didn't – I wouldn't –"

Vanessa's heart, which had been in her throat while listening to Anya's story, plummeted to her stomach.

"You didn't kill him?"

"No! God, no! He guessed about the baby, but we both agreed to not tell anyone."

Anya looked off to the side, remembering one of the last conversations she had with her father-in-law, two and a half weeks before he died.

~~~

212

A knock on her guest room door caused Anya to look up from the magazine she was reading. After a long day working at her boutique and a four-course family dinner to celebrate MaryJo's birthday – a dinner during which she and Tripp announced her pregnancy – Anya had excused herself and gone upstairs to rest.

"Yes?" she called out in reply to the knock.

The door creaked as it opened and Tom stuck his head into the room.

"Got a minute?"

Anya jumped off the bed and crossed her arms over her chest.

"I don't think that's such a –"

Her father-in-law stepped fully inside the room and shut the door behind him. "It'll just take a minute, then I'll be out of here."

Anya sighed. "What?"

"MaryJo said that you told her you're three months pregnant."

"That's right."

"Twelve weeks."

Anya nodded her head. "Three months is twelve weeks, yes."

"So it must've happened right before Tripp left for Hong Kong."

Anya shifted back and forth on her feet. "What's your point, Tom?"

"It's just that . . . I mean that's really close to –"

"Don't say it. We promised we'd never even say it."

"Are you sure?" Tom asked. "I mean, about the timing and Tripp. Are you sure?"

Anya's chin started to quiver and she blinked to hold back tears.

"You don't know," he concluded.

She closed her eyes and nodded her head up and down. "I do know," Anya whispered. "I'm ten weeks, not twelve."

Tom drew in a deep breath. "It's mine."

"You can't tell Tripp," Anya said, rushing forward to grab her father-in-law's arm. "He's so excited to be a dad. You can't tell him. Ever."

"Are you crazy? Of course I won't. I just . . . I needed to know. You can understand that, right? I needed to know."

Anya stepped back and nodded her head. "I understand. But now you need to leave. I don't want anyone seeing us alone together."

~~~

Detective Smith ran her hands through her hair, the motion catching Anya's eye and bringing her thoughts back to the present.

"If you didn't kill him," said Vanessa, "why did you think I was arresting you?"

"Because I lied. About secrets and stuff. Obstruction of justice or whatever it's called."

The detective let out a deep breath. "Yeah, well, there is that." She looked around the store. "Can your employees close up today? I'm going to need you to come with me."

"Am I still under arrest?"

"Yes."

Vanessa stood nearby while Anya feigned a family emergency and instructed her best employee to close the shop at the end of the day.

Two uniformed officers were waiting outside the store, with the front door guard having radioed the officer in the back and told him it was time to leave.

Halfway to the squad car, Vanessa stopped in her tracks. *That's it!*

"Take her to the station," she told the two officers as she started running toward her own car. "Hold her until I get there!"

Climbing into the driver's seat, Vanessa started the

214

engine with one hand while dialing her partner's phone number with the other.

"Smith," Dennis said when he answered. "What the hell is going on?"

"I'll explain later. Anya Wilson is being brought in by a couple of uniforms. False statements for sure, maybe more. But right now I need you to check flight manifests. Look public and private."

"For who?"

"Tripp Wilson. Remember how he told us he would've done anything to have a kid? Then we saw the fertility center on the credit card bill?"

"Yeah. So? His wife is pregnant. It worked."

"No, it didn't," Vanessa replied, turning on her lights and siren and speeding down the Hutchinson River Parkway in the direction of Manhattan. "The baby isn't his," she explained. "It's Tom's. Anya confirmed it, but she also denied killing him."

"And you believe her?"

"I do. We thought Anya killed Tom to cover it up, but Tripp must have gotten his test results back from the clinic and found out he couldn't have kids."

"Then his wife shows up pregnant and he finds out it was his dad. Holy shit." Dennis paused. "Hold on, hold on."

His voice faded as he talked to someone else in the precinct. "You sure? Ok, call TSA and Homeland Security. Yep, he's making a run for it."

Van Hatcher returned to the phone. "We've got a Thomas Wilson III listed on a one-way ticket to Dubai. Flight leaves from LaGuardia in an hour."

Vanessa slammed on her brakes and pulled a U-turn in the middle of the road to exit I-87 and get back on The Hutch. "I'll meet you there."

FIFTY-NINE

Detective Smith careened on two wheels into the drop-off lane at LaGuardia Airport and screeched to a stop in front of the entrance to Terminal B.

"Hey – you can't park here!" a patrol officer said.

"NYPD!" Vanessa yelled back, holding up her badge in her hand while running away from her car and into the airport.

Inside the door, Vanessa scanned the departures board to find Tripp's flight.

United Airlines to Dubai, leaving in thirty-five minutes, she read. *Concourse C.*

Not wanting to cause a scene at an airport still on edge about terrorism, Smith made a bee line for the employees' entrance to the concourse. She flashed her badge once again and ignored the sound of beeping metal detectors as she skipped the security line.

"NYPD! Move! This is an emergency!"

Slamming through a door to re-enter the public section of the airport, Vanessa sprinted down the concourse toward the last gate in the row: C14.

Shit, she thought when she got closer. *The boarding door is closed.*

"NYPD," Vanessa said with a huff, out of breath from her mad dash through the airport. "I need to –"

"Smith!"

Vanessa turned around to see Dennis racing toward her.

"Uniforms are surrounding the plane on the tarmac," he said. "There was an air marshal already on board. He's going to try to take Tripp quietly so he doesn't use any of the other passengers as hostages."

****

Unaware of the commotion outside, Tripp Wilson relaxed in seat 5B and enjoyed a glass of pre-flight champagne.

"What are we celebrating, sir?" the flight attendant asked.

"Freedom," he replied with a smile.

"Umm, excuse me, I think I'm in A," a voice said.

Tripp turned and saw a tall, skinny man with a completely-shaven head standing in the aisle next to him. "Oh, sorry about that." He unhooked his seat belt and stood up, walking out into the aisle to let the other passenger go by.

A cool flash of metal slapped against Tripp's wrist. Looking down, he saw that the 'passenger' was holding the other end of the handcuffs.

The air marshal used his free hand to reach inside his jacket pocket and show Tripp the back end of his gun.

"Thomas Wilson III," he said in a calm and quiet voice, "you're under arrest for the murder of Thomas Wilson II. Let's go. Off the plane. Don't try anything stupid," he added. "That will only make this more painful for you."

SIXTY

The interrogation room at LaGuardia was at the end of a long hall, away from the hustle and bustle of the airport. Designed for questioning asylum seekers or suspected drug traffickers, Dennis and Vanessa commandeered the room for their murder investigation.

Much to their surprise, Tripp waived his right to an attorney.

Arrogant sonofabitch probably thinks he doesn't need one, Vanessa thought.

"I'll admit it," Dennis said, looking across the table at Tom's killer. "You had me fooled."

Despite the chains and shackles around his wrists and ankles, Tripp smiled. "I had everybody fooled."

"So you admit it?"

The suspect closed his eyes let out a deep breath. "Yeah. I admit it."

"Why?" asked Vanessa. "How?"

"He slept with my wife!" Tripp yelled, slamming his hands down against the metal table. "My wife!"

"Calm down, Mr. Wilson," said Detective Van Hatcher. "Hysterics won't do you any good." After a minute, he added, "how'd you know that they slept together?"

"Remember when you two asked me about the fertility clinic? I lied. That bitch –"

"You mean your wife?"

"Yeah, her. We'd been trying to have kids ever since we got married. Nothing worked. So I went to the clinic to find out if something was medically wrong." Tripp set his jaw and spit fire from his eyes. "I'm sterile. 100%. There's zero chance I could ever father a child."

"So when Anya told you she was pregnant . . ."

"I knew the bitch had cheated on me. I figured it happened while I was in Hong Kong, so I pulled security footage at the house for those two weeks. The only guy who visited was Dad."

"It's not as if she stayed home the entire time, though," Vanessa argued. "She was at work six days a week."

Tripp nodded. "I thought about that. After all, it's not like I wanted to believe that my wife would cheat on me with my own father. But his car stayed in the driveway all night. When I asked him about seeing Anya while I was gone, he said he spent an hour working on her car and went home. He lied."

"That's still a big leap to make."

"When I left for Hong Kong, my father was a courteous, polite man. When I got back, he was a grumpy, erratic alcoholic. Before I went overseas – on a trip he arranged, by the way – he treated Anya like a second daughter. After I returned, they wouldn't even look at each other."

"So you killed him," Dennis concluded.

Tripp shrugged his shoulders. "Bastard got what he had coming to him."

SIXTY-ONE

Riding handcuffed in the back of Vanessa's government-issued Chevy Malibu, Tripp rested his head against the seat.

So close, he thought. *So damn close.*

If any number of small things had gone his way, Thomas Wilson III would've been sipping champagne on a 787 bound for Dubai – a country with no extradition treaty with the United States. There were flights nearly every hour on the hour from LaGuardia to the United Arab Emirates, but Tripp didn't make it to the airport in time for the first flight that afternoon – *stupid taxi driver*, he thought – and the next flight was fully booked. *So I had to wait. And now I'm in the back of a cop car. A shitty cop car*, Tripp thought, looking at the stained carpet in the floorboard and the torn upholstery on his seat.

Closing his eyes, the patricide reworked the entire murder scheme in his mind, trying to figure out what went wrong.

~~~

He has to be dead, Tripp thought to himself while in his office in June, shortly after Anya told him she was pregnant and he discovered the identity of the baby's father. Having decided he had no choice but to seek revenge, Tripp knew his best opportunity would be during the family's yacht cruise in late July.

If I push him overboard, he could still survive. Then I'm screwed. I can't shoot him . . . that would make noise and leave evidence, not to mention the bullet hole in his body. Tripp sighed and took another sip of bourbon, disguised in a Yeti cup on his desk. *Maybe smash him over the head with something? They'd think he hit his head on the side of the boat as he fell, right? Still no guarantee that he'd die that way, though.*

Tripp picked his iPhone up off his desk and opened the 'Settings' icon to the Wi-Fi section. "They can't trace where I go using data," he said to himself, switching his phone off of the office internet and onto 4G LTE.

The thirty-five year old business investor opened a new browser and typed 'untraceable drugs' in the search bar. The second website on the list jumped out at Tripp.

"'What Drug is the Perfect Murder Weapon?'" he read aloud. "Exactly." Clicking on the link, Tripp soon found himself reading an article written by an author of murder mysteries.

"'We have to find a drug that either leaves no metabolite trace or one that is indigenous to the body anyway'," he read. *Okay, so what is it?* "Metabolites are what's left over after the body breaks down stuff," Tripp summarized. "Got it.

"Ah, here we go," he said with a smile. "'What drug leaves no metabolite trace?' Yes. That's what I want."

Tripp scanned down to the next line. "'The simple answer is NONE.'"

Putting his phone down on his desk, Tripp looked up at the ceiling and let out a deep sigh.

"Shit."

A minute later, the would-be murderer resumed reading and discovered a few paragraphs down that there might be a drug for him after all. "Potassium chloride," he said. "The body breaks it down into stuff that already occurs naturally, so nothing foreign shows up on a tox screen. And the effects of an overdose mimic a heart attack." Tripp smiled. "Now that's what I'm talking about. I get my hands on some of the injectable kind, since that's what this guy says I need for it to work right, and that sonofabitch will be dead before he knows what hit him."

Tripp's Google search for injectable potassium chloride wasn't as successful as he'd hoped. "Damn stuff is impossible to get. Hospitals have it on lock down, with two-person passcodes and everything. Shit." Tripp ran his hand through his hair in frustration. "Maybe I could get a behind-the-scenes tour of Mount Sinai and sneak off to the pharmacy." He sighed. "Probably not. Back to square one, I guess."

Later that evening, while sitting in bed with his wife, Tripp put down the financial statements he was reading to pay attention to the TV show that Anya was watching.

"Fill me in," he said.

"It's about a famous actress who died on a boat. Nobody really knows what happened to her, but witnesses said that she mixed alcohol with sleeping pills before she fell overboard."

That's it! Tripp thought, working to hide his excitement. *Dad pops Ambien pills like they're tic-tacs. I throw a couple extra in his drink, push him overboard, and it all looks like an accident.* Despite his efforts, a small smile creased Tripp's mouth. *Exactly what that bastard deserves . . . to have his body shredded to pieces by a bunch of sharks.*

"What are you smiling about?"

Tripp jumped, startled by Anya's question.

"Huh? Oh, there was a funny cartoon going around the office today."

"What'd it say?"

"Oh, umm . . ." *Quick – think!* "What sound does a nut make when it sneezes?" Tripp asked, using the first joke that came to mind.

"I don't know. What?"

"Cashew!"

Anya rolled her eyes. "Really? That was going around Wilson|Cole today? Makes me question the security of our retirement investments."

Tripp smiled and wrapped his arm around his wife's shoulders. "Our investments are safe. Don't worry. The joke is so stupid it's funny. Just wait – it'll grow on you."

SIXTY-TWO

One month later, on the fourth night of the yacht cruise, Tripp knew it was time to put his plan into action. His little brother had already gone to sleep and he and his father were alone on the top deck.

I can't stand to spend another second on this boat with that bastard, he thought.

"Want a refill?" Tripp asked, reaching for his father's drink.

"Yeah, that'd be great. Thanks."

Tripp's hand shook as he took hold of the glass, and Tom grimaced. "Looks like the shakes have caught up to you," he commented.

"What?"

"The shaking in your hand. Happens to me sometimes . . . especially when I'm trying to eat or hold a glass or something else small. Doctor said it's called a 'familial tremor'. My dad had it too."

"I'm fine. My hands don't shake."

Tom laughed. "Eventually you'll get old, too, son. I know your generation hates to believe it, but everybody grows up. Part of growing up – and growing old – is having stuff not work like it used to."

Tripp grunted his disagreement and returned his focus to the bottle of whisky in front of him. *I don't have a fucking tremor*, he thought to himself. *I'm just a little nervous, that's all. I've never killed my father before.* Glancing over his shoulder, Tripp saw that Tom was reclined against the seat cushions and looking up at the stars.

Reaching into his shirt pocket, Tripp pulled out a plastic bag full of Ambien pills that he had ground into powder earlier that afternoon. Dumping it into his dad's drink, Tripp swirled the potion around in the glass to mix it with the scotch.

"What's taking so long? Did you have to send to the mainland for the alcohol?"

Tripp laughed. "No, sorry. Here you go," he said, walking back across the deck and handing Tom his glass. "What should we drink to?"

The elder Wilson smiled. "That new grandchild of mine. Your firstborn."

Tripp let out a deep breath and returned the smile, glad that the darkness of the night masked the wicked gleam in his eyes. "Yes," he nodded. "To my firstborn."

****

An hour later, Tripp had gone to bed and Tom was alone outside, breathing in the fresh salt air and enjoying the quiet of the night.

Standing at the side rail of the boat, Tom held his half-full glass of scotch in one hand and rested his weight on the other, swaying slightly in the drunken breeze. He leaned over to look at the water below.

"Almost looks cobalt in the moonlight," he commented, not caring that no one could hear him. The businessman sighed and nodded his head. "Father Gerry was right. This trip is good for me." Looking up at the star-filled sky, Tom smiled. "Ya done good, God," he said, imitating the yacht captain's accent. "Dis place here . . . ya done good."

Tom felt a sting in the back of his neck, a pinch, but slapped it away.

"Damn bugs," he said, shaking his head. "Only bad thing about this country. Well, that and the damn heat," he added, using his hand to wipe sweat from his brow. "Did it get hot all of a sudden?"

Tom's head felt heavy, heavy even for his drunken state, and he blinked his eyes to clear the fog in front of him.

"Woah," he said, dropping his glass over the side so he could hold onto the rail with both hands. "Oh man. I'm gonna have to talk to the cook at Staniel Cay. I think he used some bad meat or something."

Leaning farther over the rail, Tom vomited into the dark sea.

"*Ooof.*" He wiped his mouth with the back of his hand. "Definitely need to talk to the cook."

Letting go of the rail, he turned to make his way back to his cabin. Seeing three walkways instead of one, Tom picked the far-left path and stumbled forward, slamming into the rail and collapsing forward halfway over the edge of the boat.

Tom vomited again before pushing himself upright and staggering several more feet forward toward the bow of *The Arvid*. Nausea, a splitting headache, and blurred vision fought him with every step.

A push from behind threw Tom forward and his foot slipped off the edge of the deck. He fell, splitting the lower-level railing with a crushing blow to his groin.

A million tiny stars flashed on the back of his eyelids before the world went black. The last sensation Tom had was one of falling, before everything became wet and water rushed through his nose and mouth. He tried to cough, tried to scream, but it only made things worse.

Tom fought hard against gravity and the deluge of seawater attacking him from all sides. He felt the water go up his nose and down his windpipe, landing with a splash in his lungs. His chest was on fire as the remaining air tried to escape. A second later, Tom began a panicked search for oxygen. Instinct had him opening his mouth to gasp for air, but it only resulted in more water flooding in.

Fear, pain, saltwater, and scotch mixed together in Tom's body as he lashed out in the ocean, trying in vain to keep his head above the surface.

As quickly as it began, the pain stopped. The choking ended. And Tom was falling again, this time peacefully into the depths of the sea.

SIXTY-THREE

"Good evening and welcome to Channel 3 News at 7. I'm Fred Taylor. We start tonight with a stunning turn of events in the death of millionaire Thomas Wilson II. For the story, let's head up to Anthony Quinn, who is standing by in the Upper East. Anthony?"

"Thanks Fred. I'm back here tonight in front of the Wilson's brownstone on East 63rd Street, where Tom Wilson's widow still lives. We first brought you this story back in early August when the millionaire investment banker went missing aboard his yacht and was later found dead in the Caribbean Sea. You'll recall that, after a lengthy investigation, the NYPD declared Mr. Wilson's death to be an accident. In a move no one saw coming, today the NPYD announced that Thomas Wilson III, the victim's son, confessed to killing his father. Police are being tight-lipped about the circumstances surrounding his confession," the reporter added, "but a source tells me that the murder may have been the result of an affair between the victim and his son's wife. Back to you, Fred."

In the studio, the veteran anchorman sat silent, his jaw dropped in shock.

A producer waved his arms and jumped up and down to get Fred's attention.

"Right. Wow. Okay. Apparently we'll have more on that angle of the story on our broadcast at eleven. So stay tuned . . . I know I will."

After the producer yelled 'cut', the anchorman took out his earpiece and turned to face his colleague.

"Seriously? He slept with his own daughter-in-law? How fucked up is that?"

****

226

At the Fifth Precinct in Chinatown, the Assistant District Attorney assigned to the Wilson case walked up to stand next to Vanessa. Both women looked through a large two-way mirror and listened as Detective Van Hatcher grilled Tripp on the details of his confession.

"Seriously?" the prosecutor asked. "He slept with his own daughter-in-law? How fucked up is that?"

Vanessa shook her head. "Nothing surprises me anymore with this family."

Inside the witness box, Dennis stood with his hands on his hips and trained a watchful eye on the perp sitting in front of him.

"Is there any way . . ." Tripp stopped his question mid-sentence.

"Is there any way what?"

"Is there any way to keep the reason quiet? I know my confession will be public, but can't you blame it on a drunken argument about work or something like that?"

Dennis laughed. "You kill your own father, lie about it for months, only confess after we catch you at LaGuardia trying to flee the country, and now you want me to help you cover it all up? You've got some serious nerve, man. Besides, it's too late. Secret's out."

Tripp sighed and rested his head in his shackled hands.

"This will destroy my mom. Ryan will never recover from it. He idolizes Dad. He's dedicated his whole life to making him proud. When he hears the truth . . ."

"Tell me something, Mr. Wilson," Dennis replied. "If you're so worried about the truth coming out, so worried about you mom and brother's well-being, why wouldn't you just let your dad live? Why kill him? The truth about what he did was obviously eating him alive. Why not let him suffer and live with that while the rest of your family went undisturbed?"

Tripp's eyes glassed over and, on the other side of the mirror, Vanessa shivered from the coldness of his stare.

"I need a child. An heir. And a child needs a mother. But one of them had to pay." Tripp lowered his voice to a near-whisper. "One of them had to pay for what they did."

****

"We've got the confession?" the ADA asked after Dennis emerged from the interview.

"Signed, sealed, and delivered," he replied, handing the piece of paper to the prosecutor.

Vanessa looked past her two colleagues to see Tripp leaning back in his chair and staring at the ceiling. "I still can't believe it was him. Of all the Wilsons . . . I never would've guessed Tripp."

"Except you did guess it," her partner corrected her.

"Only after Anya gave me her side of the story – as disgusting as that was."

"I came in late to the interview," said the district attorney. "How'd he do it? Fit of rage and pushed him overboard?"

Dennis shook his head. "The sonofabitch planned it. He looked up different ways to kill his dad. Even did the research on his phone using data, not WiFi, so we wouldn't be able to trace the searches on an IP address."

"Smart."

"Yep. He almost went the poison route. Apparently injectable potassium chloride is untraceable and mimics the effects of a heart attack."

Vanessa's eyes grew wide. "Tom Wilson's autopsy showed signs of cardiac arrest."

"That wasn't from poisoning. Tripp couldn't get his hands on any potassium chloride without someone finding out what he was up to. He even went so far as to use his family's seat on the board at Mount Sinai to arrange a hospital tour, thinking that he could sneak off at some point and steal some from the pharmacy." Dennis paused. "Also not a bad idea. It might've worked a few years ago. But there have been so many stories recently about hospital staff stealing drugs that they've really clamped down on access."

"So how'd he do it?" asked the prosecutor.

"Slipped a bunch of Ambien into his drink. It doubled the effect of both – made him extra tired and extra drunk. Tripp said he barely had to push Tom at all to make him fall overboard."

SIXTY-FOUR

His interview work complete, Dennis shook hands with the Assistant District Attorney and headed toward his desk at the other end of the building.

"Detective Van Hatcher," Joe Tumlin said, jogging to catch up to him.

"Yes?"

"I wanted to make sure there are no hard feelings about this case," said the Wilson family attorney. "I know I clammed up on you about things that would've made your investigation easier, but I wouldn't be much of a lawyer if I didn't keep the confidences of my clients."

Dennis nodded his head. "Understood. I don't like it, but I understand it. Tell me something, though. Knowing what you knew about the changes to the will, is this the outcome you expected?"

The lawyer sighed and put his hands in his pockets. "I didn't know what outcome to expect, to tell you the truth. I still don't feel very comfortable talking to you about a privileged conversation, but I guess it's all out in the open now." He paused. "I knew that Tom was carrying around a very big, very heavy secret. When he died and I heard that you guys were going to investigate, I suspected that his secret was the motive for the murder. I didn't have a clue as to *who* did it, but I had a pretty solid guess as to *why*."

~~~

Two weeks before the Wilsons' annual Caribbean vacation, Tom called his attorney to arrange a meeting.

Strange that he made the appointment himself, the lawyer thought, accustomed to Mr. Wilson's assistant making such a call for him.

On the day of the appointment, Tom arrived looking

disheveled and unkempt. His $10,000 suit was wrinkled and off-center, his gray hair was ruffled, and a day-old beard loomed over his usually clean-shaven face.

"Come on in, Mr. Wilson. Have a seat. Can I get you anything to drink?"

"Whisky would be wonderful."

"I've got water and soda," his attorney replied, bending over to reach into a small refrigerator beside his desk.

"Water, please."

"So," Tumlin said, passing the bottle of water to his client and sitting down in his own chair, "how've you been?"

Tom ran his hand through his hair. "Uh, alright I guess. Busy. As always."

Joe looked at his client with a worried smile. "I understand. What can I do for you?"

Tom shifted in his seat and loosened his tie, almost as if it were a noose around his neck. "I, uh, I have some questions about my will."

"Okay. Shoot."

"As things are now," Tom began, "I leave most of it to MaryJo, various items to certain charities, and the rest is divided among my three kids."

"That's correct," his attorney replied, having read the document that morning to refresh his memory. *What's he so nervous about?* he wondered.

"So, uh, when could or what would have to happen for someone to be able to challenge its validity?"

"I'm not sure I follow." On a hunch, Tumlin added: "anything you tell me is protected by confidentiality."

Tom sighed. "Is it that obvious?"

"If the worry lines on your face didn't give it away, the request for whisky at 10am definitely would have."

"Right. Well, thing is . . . the thing is that I don't have three kids. I have four. Or I will have four."

Three decades as a trusts and estates attorney in Manhattan enabled Joe Tumlin to process the bombshell

231

without the slightest flinch on his face. Illegitimate children, second families, and hidden money were nothing new to him. Even if they were a surprise to be coming from the estimable Tom Wilson.

"Mistress?" he asked.

"No. No mistress. A one-time thing. A very drunken, huge mistake one-time thing. *Huge* mistake."

"Now your concern is that this new child or the child's mother will attempt to gain a portion of your estate?"

"Eh, not exactly."

"This would go a lot more smoothly, and my advice would be a lot better, if you'd tell me the whole story."

"To then have my family force you to tell them after I die? No thanks."

Tumlin shook his head. "No, that's not how it works. Confidentiality survives death."

"Really?"

"Really. So . . . what's going on here?"

~~~

"Will you at least now admit to me that he told you the whole story?" asked Dennis, still standing beside Joe Tumlin in the hallway of the 5th Precinct. "I read the rule. You can't divulge any secrets that would disparage Tom Wilson's memory. Trust me, man, that ship has sailed. Pun intended."

"You're right. Tom's epic fall from grace is complete . . . his reputation can't drop any lower than it is now." The lawyer took a deep breath. "Yes, he told me the whole story. And, since you read the rule, you understand why I couldn't reveal anything to you."

"Yeah," Dennis nodded. "I would definitely say that impregnating his daughter-in-law is something that would disparage his memory."

"If I hadn't heard it straight from him, I never would've believed it. There are some messed up people in this world."

Dennis looked down the hall and saw Tripp still sitting in the interview room, handcuffed and awaiting transport to jail. "There certainly are," he replied. "There certainly are."

SIXTY-FIVE

A few days later in Rhode Island, St. George's was finishing up a tennis match against its archrival, Middlesex.

Ryan Wilson, playing #2 singles, wiped his face with a towel and tossed it into the large bin by the courts. The team manager would wash all of the laundry later.

"Great win," a male voice called out from the bleachers.

Ryan turned and saw Charles Cole, his dad's business partner, leaning against the fence.

"Mr. Cole. Hi."

Charles smiled. "Hi to you. Congratulations," he said, nodding his head toward the court. "You were great out there."

"Thanks. I umm . . ." Ryan paused and looked around the tennis center. "Is my mom here or something?"

"What? No."

"Oh, okay." Ryan returned his focus to packing up his tennis gear, not sure why Mr. Cole would be at his school.

"I thought maybe we could grab some coffee if you have a minute," the visitor offered.

So he does want something from me. "Sure," Ryan said. "There's a coffee shop about a block outside of the front gates. Purgatory's. Let me hit the showers real quick so I don't smell, and then I'll meet you there. Does that work?"

Charles nodded. "Yep. Sounds great. I'll see you there."

Thirty minutes later, the high school sophomore had showered and changed into khakis, sneakers, and a red hoodie sweatshirt with 'St. George's Tennis' emblazoned on the front. He hopped on his bike and pedaled down the street toward the local student hangout, named after the road where it – and the school – were located.

Mr. Cole was there waiting, having already grabbed a table in the corner.

"Do you want anything?" he asked, gesturing toward the

counter.

"No thanks," Ryan replied, pulling a water bottle out of his backpack. "I need to rehydrate after the match."

Charles shook his head. "Man, things are different now. Back when I was playing sports, they made us eat salt tablets and said that water made us weak. Now you kids are like well-oiled machines with your organic food and 'proper hydration'."

Ryan shrugged his shoulders as he took a large sip of water. "Just doing what Coach tells us." He paused. "Is there something I can help you with, Mr. Cole?"

"No. Why do you ask?"

"No offense, but it's kinda weird you showing up here like this. I thought maybe your kid was gonna apply here and you wanted to check it out, but then I remembered you don't have kids, right?"

Charles took a deep breath. "Actually, that's what I wanted to talk to you about."

"Kids?"

"Yeah." He rubbed a hand through his hair. "Not kids per se. But, well . . . I'm sorry. I'm screwing this up."

Ryan looked at his visitor in confusion. "Screwing what up?"

"I know you've been going through some tough stuff this year," Mr. Cole began. "With what happened to your dad, and then finding out about Tripp and Anya."

Ryan sucked in a breath through gritted teeth. What happened on the boat and between his dad and Anya was terrible, to be sure, but it was a family matter. *None of his business*, he thought.

When the teenager didn't respond, Charles continued: "it's just that I don't want you to think you've somehow inherited any kind of weird genes or anything like that."

Ryan glared at his father's business partner. "You think my family is genetically deformed? That because my dad had an affair and my brother killed him that I'm somehow destined to be a fuck up too?"

Several other patrons in the coffee shop turned to look at Charles and Ryan.

"Shhh," Charles whispered.

"Don't 'shhh' me, old man. This is my school. My turf. *My family.*"

Charles put his hands up in front of him. "I'm sorry. Of course. I didn't meant to 'shhh' you." He sighed and looked down at his cup of coffee. "Look, all I wanted to say is that I'm here for you if you ever need anything. Tom and your mom and I go way back and, well . . . I'm here for you."

Ryan nodded his head. "Thanks. And thanks for driving all the way up here. But you really didn't need to. Commissioner Clark has already taken over father-figure duties, so you're off the hook."

****

Fifteen minutes later, after pedaling back to his dorm, Ryan Wilson closed his door and grabbed his cell phone out of his backpack.

MaryJo picked up on the third ring.

"Hey honey, this is a surprise. Is everything okay?"

"What the hell happened between you and Charles Cole?"

MaryJo choked on her coffee.

"W-what?"

"What the hell happened between you and Charles Cole?"

"I don't know what you're talking about," she lied. *Well, sort of. He could be talking about something totally random.*

"Mr. Cole came to see me today," Ryan said. "Wanted to talk after my match."

MaryJo's face turned white. "He . . . he came to see you? What did he say?"

"That he's 'here for me'," Ryan answered, making air

236

quotes with his fingers. "Dude was totally creepy about it too. Said he and Dad were close, blah blah blah. And he's 'here for me'. Kept saying that over and over."

"Well, honey, I think that was a very kind gesture. He and your father were business partners for a long time, and it's nice of him to want to help support our family now that your dad is gone."

On the other end of the line, Ryan shook his head. *I'm not buying it.*

"Dad slept with Anya and my niece or nephew will actually be my brother or sister," he blurted out. "Is Charles Cole really my father?"

MaryJo's whole body went still, sending her coffee cup crashing to the floor.

Hearing the noise, Ryan let out a low growl. "I knew it. What. the. fuck," he said, emphasizing each word. "Shit man, no wonder he wanted me to know that I wasn't genetically deformed like the rest of the Wilsons."

"He said that?"

"More or less. I can't . . . I don't even . . . ahhhhh. What else isn't true, huh? Am I your son? Is Tripp my brother? Does Kay really belong to the commissioner? Seriously, Mom. How many of Dad's friends did you sleep with?"

MaryJo started to sob and tears rolled down her cheeks. "I'm so sorry, honey. I'm so, so sorry. Your father was working long hours trying to make the company a success. Charles was too – they all were during those years. They made a couple of bad investments and had to right the ship. But it was an obsession for your father."

"Tom," Ryan corrected. "He's not my father."

MaryJo covered her eyes with her hand and bit her lip in a futile effort to stop the tears from streaming down her face.

"Were you ever going to tell me?" Ryan asked, his voice laced with pain.

"I didn't know for sure. I wondered, but I didn't know for sure. Not until they ran the bloodwork in the autopsy for

237

genetic malformities. You didn't match either of us, and that's when I knew."

Ryan felt his own lower lip begin to quiver.

"I'm so sorry, honey," MaryJo repeated. "I'm so, so sorry."

SIXTY-SIX

At McSorley's in Manhattan, Dennis sat in his favorite corner booth surrounded by a pitcher of beer and an extra-large basket of french fries.

"This seat taken?" his partner asked as she walked up, herself holding another pitcher and a fresh glass.

"What are you doing here? Go home. See your husband."

"He's staying at his brother's for a while," Vanessa replied, sliding into the other side of the booth.

"Everything alright?"

Vanessa ignored the question. "French fries and beer?" she asked, eyeing the basket in the middle of the table. "I was expecting chocolate cake and tequila."

Dennis nodded and ran his hand over his face, the strain of the last several days showing. "I know, I know. We got our man so I should be celebrating."

"But . . ."

Van Hatcher sighed. "This one doesn't feel like a win, you know? It seems like the family would've been better off if it stayed listed as an accident. What they didn't know couldn't hurt them." He shrugged his shoulders and refilled his glass of beer. "I dunno. Maybe I've been at this too long. Letting cases get to me like this one did."

Vanessa popped a fry into her mouth and shook her head. "Nuh uh. You haven't been at it too long. This case got to all of us. All that proves is that you're human."

"Exactly. Humanity'll get you killed in a job like this." He took another long drink of beer. "If this family was even halfway normal, Tripp would've gotten away with it. Add the sleeping pills to the alcohol, Tom gets drunk, goes overboard, the end. Natalie Wood part two. But the wife had the affair with the business partner and the son-in-law had the imminent bankruptcy, and then the vic goes and knocks up his own daughter-in-law."

A hint of a smile crossed Vanessa's face. "The Wilsons are WAF," she said, using Ryan's favorite term.

Her partner laughed. "Totally WAF. That's what did him in. They went full WAF and he got caught."

"Never go full WAF."

"Cheers to that," Dennis replied, raising his glass. "To having a normal, middle-class life . . . and never ending up like the Wilson family."

EPILOGUE

Eight months after Thomas II's body was found floating in the Caribbean, and five months after Thomas III pled guilty to drugging and murdering his father, the remaining members of the Wilson family were still struggling to adapt to their new normal.

Kay and Luke were no longer on the edge of bankruptcy, with her inheritance settling Luke's debts and even allowing them to buy back some of the antiques they auctioned off in order to pay bills. The Eckerselys were, however, on the edge of divorce. The stress of Tom's murder investigation combined with the shock of Tripp's confession made the entire Wilson clan the subject of gossip, derision, and scorn in New York society – and had exposed the worst sides of Kay and Luke's selfish personalities.

To escape the fighting, Madison and Harper were spending an increasing amount of time at their grandmother's townhouse. MaryJo relished the opportunity to spend time with the girls and viewed them as the family's last best hope for a new beginning. Once the darling of Manhattan's elite, MaryJo also enjoyed having her granddaughters around because they gave her someone to talk to. In a city where appearances and reputation meant everything, very few were willing to risk being seen with the widow of an adulterer and mother of a murderer.

The police commissioner and his wife, Derrick and Cindy Clark, ignored the calls to abandon their friend and were still frequent visitors at the mansion on East 63rd. Derrick had even ventured to Philadelphia a few times to visit Anya and her newborn son. He couldn't quite explain it, but Clark felt a duty to watch over his best friend's child – even given the circumstances under which young Noah entered the world. In the irony of ironies, the infant had inherited not only his small enumerated portion of Tom's estate but also Tripp's larger share, since state law prohibited Tripp from profiting off his crime.

Commissioner Clark also felt compelled to look out for

243

Ryan, the teenager whose world was turned inside-out and upside-down in the span of four short months. *First his dad died,* Derrick thought, *then he found out that his brother killed his dad because his dad slept with his brother's wife. And, to top it all off, he discovered that Tom Wilson wasn't his father after all.* The commissioner shook his head. *It's amazing the boy hasn't gone completely insane.*

After a brief spell of rebellious wandering, Ryan had indeed settled back into life at St. George's. Other students gossiped and snickered for a little while, but Ryan X, as he had taken to calling himself – "I'm not a Wilson and I'm not a Cole," he argued – soon discovered one of the perks of attending an elite New England boarding school: the vast majority of his classmates also had family secrets of which they were ashamed. Mutually assured destruction meant that Ryan X was not a pariah for long.

That spring, he declined several invitations from his friends to join them on trips to Aspen, St. Bart's, and Lake Como.

I WANT TO TAKE *THE ARVID* OUT FOR SPRING BREAK, Ryan told his mom via text.

WHAT? NO.

COME ON, MOM. I ALREADY EMAILED SHIP AND HE SAID IT WAS OKAY.

At home in Manhattan, MaryJo sighed and shook her head. After her husband's death, the family decided to sell their yacht. *Too many bad memories,* she thought. But with no one willing to purchase a boat on which a man died and the Wilsons being eager to sell it quickly, the only buyer who could be found was its previous owner: Captain Blankenship Jones. Ship rented the yacht went he felt like company and sailed alone when he didn't, without the least bit of bother about the Wilsons' troubles. *Their life, their problem. No need ta make it my problem too,* he reasoned.

MaryJo's phone buzzed again.

SHIP SAID THAT IF IT'S OKAY WITH YOU THEN IT'S OKAY

244

WITH HIM. PLEASE? Ryan asked, including a praying hands emoji at the end.

Letting out a deep breath, Mrs. Wilson pulled up her list of recent calls and pressed on her son's name.

"Why in the world would you want to spend a second on that infernal boat, let alone an entire week?"

"Because I like it," Ryan replied. "The boat didn't kill Dad . . . err, Tom. It's not *The Arvid*'s fault that her owners were a bunch of lunatics."

MaryJo chose to ignore the lunatics remark.

"I don't see how you would have any fun on there by yourself," she argued.

"I won't be by myself. Ship and the rest of the crew will be aboard. Besides, he promised to teach me how to work everything. It'll be good for me, Mom," Ryan said. "Fresh air and warm sunshine and all that crap."

"Okay, fine. But do what Ship tells you. If it gets to be too much for you, to be back in the Bahamas or back on the boat, call me. I'll fly you home."

"Yes! Sweet! Thanks Mom! Don't worry – it won't be too much. It's gonna be perfect."

****

On his first night aboard *The Arvid* since his father died on it eight months earlier, Ryan went into the yacht's master bedroom and closed and locked the door behind him.

Placing Tom's black weekender bag on the bed, Ryan got down on the floor on his stomach and stuck both arms under the mattress. After a couple of tugs, he succeeded in dislodging a medium-sized wooden box.

"Here we go," Ryan said, pulling the box out from under the bed. "Jackpot."

Inside was Tom's emergency supply of scotch: three 25-year Macallans, a 50-year Glenfiddich, and a 50-year Balvenie. The latter two cost over $20,000 each, which made them all the more attractive to the sixteen year old boy.

Shoving all of the bottles in the black carryall, Ryan zipped the bag closed, threw it over his shoulder, and walked back to the door.

"Party time, Pops," he said.

Grabbing his tennis racket off the couch as he passed through the living room, the young Mr. Wilson/Cole/X climbed the spiral staircase to the top deck and settled onto the open-air couch.

An hour later, half a bottle of whisky was in Ryan's stomach. Another hour after that, the Macallan was oozing out of his pores.

"Here you go, Pops, since you love tennis so much," Ryan said, tossing his racket over the railing. "Isn't that 'bitchin'?"

Ryan unscrewed the bottle of Balvenie and took a swig. "Thirsty? Have some," he said, pouring the $30,000 single-malt whisky into the sea. "Drink up, old man. Driiiiiiiiink it on up."

After emptying the entire contents of the boat's liquor cabinet into the water, Ryan stumbled downstairs to the master bedroom and fell face-first onto the bed. A few minutes later, he rolled over to look at the ceiling that his mom had painted to look like the night sky.

"Figures," he thought aloud. "She's on a boat in the middle of the damn ocean and she'd rather look at a fake sky than go outside and see the real thing.

"'Appearances matter'," Ryan said, imitating his mom's high-pitched voice. "'They're not supposed to, but people judge books by their covers all the time.'" The teenager scoffed. "As long as everything appears to be perfect, who gives a shit what the truth is, right?"

****

The next morning, when Ryan hadn't emerged from his

room by ten o'clock, Ship knocked on the bedroom door.

"Ryan? Ya awake? It's already ten. I know ya said ya wanted ta go fishin' today an' the best ones will have –"

Ship stopped mid-sentence. Ryan wasn't in his bedroom. "Marcelo! Have ya seen Ryan?"

The Arvid's first mate walked down the hall and shook his head. "Nah, not since last night. He's not in there sleepin'?"

Ship shook his head and scanned the room with his eyes. Seeing an envelope on the dressing table, the captain walked over and picked it up.

His heart dropped to his stomach as he tore open the paper. Inside was a note, handwritten in perfect cursive:

Ship,
Don't bother looking for me. I wore scuba belts to make sure I sank, and I put steak in my pockets so the sharks will get me before SAR can.

Mom,
You always told me I would end up just like Dad. As usual, you were right.

Ryan

Please write a review online and let Danielle know your thoughts!

ABOUT THE AUTHOR

Danielle knew she was born to be a writer at age four when she entertained an entire emergency room with the – false – story of how she was adopted. *Secrets of the Deep* is Danielle's sixth novel. She is a graduate of Georgetown University (Go Hoyas!) and Harvard Law School. Danielle lives in Georgia with her chocolate lab, Gus.

Find out more about Danielle and her books on her website: www.daniellesingleton.com.

Follow Danielle on Twitter: @auntdanwrites

Like Danielle's Facebook page: www.facebook.com/singletondanielle

Read Danielle's blog: www.daniellesingleton.wordpress.com

86327209R00144

Made in the USA
San Bernardino, CA
28 August 2018